Carlo Gébler's n
Work and Play. Hi
Through Cuba, w
Enniskillen, *A C*
1991. He lives in

'Written with taut exa
scale turbulences; the Irish Troubles,
of the First and Second World Wars, the Hungar
uprising of 1956' *Sunday Times*

'Fascinating and impressive' *Standard*

'Cunningly compelling . . . Mr Gébler is a bit of a
magician' *Sunday Press*

'A novel of some stature' *Observer*

Also by Carlo Gébler in Abacus:

DRIVING THROUGH CUBA

CARLO GÉBLER

Malachy and his Family

An *Abacus* Book

First published in Great Britain by
Hamish Hamilton Ltd 1990

Published in Abacus by Sphere Books Ltd 1991

Copyright © Carlo Gébler 1990

Printed and bound in Great Britain by
Cox & Wyman Ltd, Reading

ISBN 0 349 10194 9

Sphere Books Ltd
A Division of
Macdonald & Co (Publishers) Ltd
Orbit House
1 New Fetter Lane
London EC4A 1AR
A member of Maxwell Macmillan Pergamon Publishing Corporation

To Tyga

Acknowledgements

I would like to thank Mr Stephen Barlay for his advice on the historical background. I would also like to thank Dr Keith Hawton. Any mistakes of course are my own.

Carlo Gébler

Adam has eaten the apple and our teeth ache from it

Hungarian proverb

Diary, Hampton Wick

I closed the front door and followed the others across the gravel to the car. I got into the front passenger seat and my half-brother got behind the wheel. We are both called Malachy. This could have made for a very complicated childhood but this never arose as we grew up on different continents.

It was three weeks since I'd arrived to stay with the O'Neills and it was his twenty-fifth birthday. My father had lent us his car and we were setting out, five of us, to celebrate.

The others were in the back of course. First, my half-sister Eva. Second, the young man she had brought along, I guessed a boyfriend, whom I hadn't met before. He had been introduced to me as Peake. I didn't like him. Last, was Avril, Eva's best friend. She was small, a tiny bit plump and her nose was pointed. Our destination was a new club, The Badhouse, and we had tickets to see a band, The Butthole Surfers.

We drove slowly along Dyson Avenue, just in case my father was watching us from the house. Ridged cloud lay above us like a lid across the sky. I looked at the cherry trees as we passed them one by one.

"Wee-how …" shouted Malachy at the wheel, after we had turned the corner. He leapt from his seat upwards and knocked his head against the roof. "… A night on the town." He began to speed up.

"Malachy, calm down," ordered Peake, "*tranquillo*."

"Wee-how." Malachy leapt up again.

"He's at an impressionable age," said Eva.

"He's like a young puppy," said Peake.

"More like a young salmon, wee-how," he leapt from the

driver's seat again, "is actually how I see myself."

Avril laughed and asked, "Do you want me to drive?"

Eva said, "It's been an awful summer. I wish the sun would shine more."

"Absolutely frightful," said Peake in the way he imagined an ancient dowager spoke.

He and Eva began to talk between themselves. I stared out of the window. There was an atmosphere of prosperity about the suburb. Gateposts and gable walls and fence posts newly painted. Clipped lawns and tidy flowerbeds and crazy paving pathways with no weeds in the cracks. Garages with their doors open and new cars sat beside huge barbecues which could be wheeled about on castors, and neatly rolled lengths of garden hose.

In the next section of the city there were playing fields surrounded by green railings where small figures ran up and down, and distant views of blocks of flats with a few lights showing behind the windows, and long stretches of straight carriageway with cars and lorries speeding along.

At Cherry Blossom corner we climbed up a steep ramp onto a curving stretch of road that was the width of a single car.

I heard Eva saying, "I love this bit. It's like the Big Dipper," and then I lost her conversation again.

A gust of wind shook the car. The motorway was below us, like a dark roll of unfurled material, vehicles moving along it. It was overlooked by an ugly building with chocolate-coloured glass.

A hundred feet further on we dropped down to the ground again. The houses were small and they did not look prosperous despite the addition of bow windows and panelled doors. Cars were smaller and older. Pedestrians moved more hurriedly.

We passed a huge hospital with a flower seller sitting outside. He had turned on the electric light attached to the side of his stall. It was beginning to get dark and the buildings appeared to be glowing. It was as if they had soaked up light all day, and now dusk had come, it was all seeping out.

A car came up behind with its horn honking furiously. It started to pass, its aerial was arching back in the wind and a squirrel's tail fluttering madly from the wing mirror. White faces with short hair stared at us through the side windows and one of the passengers raised his middle index finger.

"Up your arse you cunts," said Peake, speaking in his dowager's voice again, "with a broken bottle."

He smiled out falsely through the window and gave a false little wave, like a bored celebrity going through the motions before a crowd.

The car overtook and pulled in front of us. There were red lights on the back shelf, an enormous fender, and two plastic thongs dangling underneath to the tarmac. I wondered if they were going to start pumping their brakes, accelerating and then abruptly slowing down again. The muscles in my thighs started to tremble slightly and I could feel my stomach tightening.

"Stupid young kids," said Avril.

I looked first at the plastic tails wiggling below, and then through the back windscreen at the heads which I could just make out moving inside. I was certain they were talking about what they could do to get at us. Then a cloud of exhaust burst from the back and the car sped away.

We turned a sharp corner and came to an even poorer part of the city. There were shops selling motor accessories, saris, and in a café a big brown mound of kebab meat slowly turned behind a half-fogged window. An Indian family struggled with their shopping in bulging plastic bags, and a woman had piled her groceries on to her pram around her child. The gutters were filled with rubbish and at the end of the road, on a grimy stretch of green, tramps lay on the grass amongst the rubbish.

Following signs, *Central London*, we turned on to a motorway running at roof-top level. In the streets below us, cars crawled, their headlamps at half-beam.

We descended by a curving ramp, skirted the edge of Paddington station and came eventually to a concrete roundabout. A black man stood in the middle, his head tilted back, shouting at the sky. Behind him loomed an enormous billboard advertising the opening of a new supermarket with a picture of a swinging champagne bottle.

I turned my head to look up at the sky myself but at that moment we disappeared into a tunnel where the roof was darkened with exhaust fumes.

"That's disgusting," said Malachy, looking into the rear-view mirror. "You're spoiling Avril's evening."

I couldn't stop myself turning round to see. Eva, her lips pursed, was loudly kissing her boyfriend on his cheek. The intention was to leave the impression of her lipstick there. In the gap between the seats, her knees were turned towards me, bare and brown. Peake had slipped his hand just underneath the hem of her skirt and it lay there on her thigh, draped in black. It looked like it belonged anywhere on her.

"You're meant to be past all that snogging stuff at your age," Malachy continued. "How about some adult conversation? Entertaining the driver?"

When I'd first arrived I hadn't followed. It was only now I'd been with them for a while, I was beginning to understand the tone of brother and sister. When they sparred, they meant the very opposite of what they said, which was very confusing for this plain speaker.

"What do you want to talk about?" asked Eva, bringing her shining face forward and winking at me. There was lipstick on the crease between her lip and her chin. "Or shall we play I Spy. I spy with my little eye – this is going to be difficult, isn't it Avril? – something beginning with 'R', four letters, and ending in 'D'."

"Start looking up Willesden High street," Malachy said and he passed back the *A–Z* to her.

Darkness was falling outside. A cluster of teenagers stood on a corner eating chips from paper bags. We passed a brightly lit shop with a sign in the window, *Home Video Two chillers for a £1 a nite. Limited.* In a Halal butcher's a man in a blood-splattered coat raised a cleaver over a huge carcass. The faces in the streets, black and white, all struck me as worried.

"Let's get some drink."

Malachy stopped and handed me a ten-pound note.

"Get two halves of Bell's."

I got out and went towards a supermarket barricaded with a heavy grille. There was the bitter, salty taste of stale pee in the air.

Inside the door, an Indian with bloodshot eyes stared at me suspiciously. A huge notice warned patrons of the security cameras. All shoplifters, it added, would be prosecuted.

The alcohol was on the shelves behind the cash till. I joined the back of the queue.

"If you don't want to buy then just leave."

It was the man with the bloodshot eyes. He was addressing two schoolgirls I'd noticed browsing. He escorted them to the door and then resumed his position as a human screen on the threshold.

It was hard to judge the age of the man at the head of the queue. He had long grey hair tied in a pony tail and a dog on a lead of brown string. He asked for a bottle of Thunderbird, had the right money in coppers, and carried his purchase away wrapped in a brown paper bag.

He was followed by a woman with large gold hoop earrings and a creased face. She was with a small child in a push chair. She had tea bags, sugar, milk and white bread in a wire basket. The prices were rung up.

"Oh, lord," she said, and looked into her open purse in disbelief. "It's more than I've got."

"I'm going to have to alter the roll," complained the woman in the sari behind the till.

The man with her – he loaded the customers' carrier bags – spoke to her in Hindi. A fourth figure appeared with a key to unlock the drawer and release the till roll. The man with the bloodshot eyes took away the tea bags and returned with a smaller, cheaper box.

"I'm sorry," said the woman.

"Just check you have the right money next time," he said dourly.

The child was beginning to whine.

Four more customers later, my turn came. I bought the whisky and as I was hurrying towards the door, the man with the bloodshot eyes took me completely by surprise and said, "Good night, sir."

In the car we drove around the corner and stopped in a side street beside Indo-Pak Grocers. It was boarded up and the top half was covered in soot.

"Fire bombed," Peake said sarcastically.

Malachy unscrewed the top of one of the halves and started to drink. I was next. The whisky had a burnt taste and as soon as it trickled into my stomach I could feel it warming me. I handed the bottle on to Avril.

When it was gone, we drove to Willesden and parked near the

club.

There were several police on the pavement and a large patrol van parked nearby. Standing around were about thirty or forty people of our age, smoking and talking. The males were mostly in leather jackets and motorcycle boots. There were a few girls in short tartan kilts and torn fishnets.

We turned into the passageway which ran along the side of the club. At the other end there were a crowd of young people, quite a large crowd of them, pushing and jostling around the entrance of The Badhouse.

Half-way down a mesh gate divided the passage. One of the three policemen on the far side said,

"Do you have tickets?"

"Yes."

"Can I see them?"

Malachy showed him our five green tickets.

"I'm going to have to ask you to wait here for a while," the policeman said. "There are a large number of people down by the door without tickets, and we want them to disperse before we let anyone else down."

We took a couple of steps back.

"Have you got the other bottle of whisky?" asked Eva quietly.

"It's in my pocket," said her brother.

"Do you think you should get rid of it?" asked Avril.

"There's nothing I can do about it now."

"Do you think we'll be searched?" asked Peake, sounding faintly nervous.

"They've got so many other things to worry about up there," said Malachy, "I doubt they'll be asking us to turn our pockets out."

A huge man barged past and tried to push open the gate.

"Ticket holder," he said in a tone which mixed irritation with confidence despite his foreign accent.

"Sorry, you'll have to wait," said the policeman. There was an edge to his voice.

The young man grunted and moved his enormous frame half a step back.

"You're standing on my toe," Eva said to him.

I looked down and so did he and so did Avril, Malachy and Peake. The heel of the stranger's motorcycle boot with its silver spur had just nipped the point of Eva's suede winklepicker.

"Sorry," he said and shifted his foot.

"We were at the head of the queue," said Eva.

He said nothing but just stood there with his back to us and started rolling himself a cigarette. Avril stuck her tongue out at his shoulder blades. He had three blondish rats' tails snaking over his motorcycle jacket collar, and a star tattooed on his right earlobe. I could see how it was possible to hate someone based entirely on the experience of seeing them from behind.

More and more people came up. After a while the police said we could all go through although the mob was still at the end, pressed around the entrance.

We got to the bottom of the passage and stood at the back of the crowd. We didn't want to get too close. The others who followed up behind us didn't seem so reticent. We were jostled forward and before very long we were not on the edge of the crowd but in the middle. Ahead of me I could see the entrance of The Badhouse at the top of a short flight of steps. There were three policemen with glum expressions standing there. There was also a man in a suit who had a beard.

"Listen," he said, "will those of you without tickets just back off and go home. There are no tickets left for the Buttholes."

"I fucking well rang up here today and I was told there were tickets. You've been wasting my time, you cunt."

The speaker was a small girl somewhere at the front. All I could see of her was her purple-dyed hair as she bobbed up and down.

"Listen," the man in the suit replied. "If you'd got here at six you'd have got a ticket but it's ten o'clock now and they're gone. Can I please appeal to those without tickets to move back and let those with tickets come in."

"There're only a few of us without tickets here," shouted a man with ginger hair who also wore a leather jacket. "You're an Irishman and so I am," he continued, "and I want to know, Where's your fucking Celtic solidarity?"

There was a muted round of applause from the crowd.

"There are no more tickets. We cannot let you in because it is illegal to let you in ..."

The crowd groaned and pressed forward, carrying us with them. The girl with purple hair started protesting again about the waste of her time. As more people came up from behind, I could feel myself being pressed against Avril and Eva and Malachy and Peake, and against the people around us. There was a strong smell of leather because everyone seemed to be in a leather jacket, and coming from somewhere, the sweet smell of marijuana.

"Stand aside please."

A police sergeant in a peaked cap forced his way through with enormous difficulty and climbed on to the steps. He was holding a clipboard.

"I'm sorry, ladies and gentlemen, but will those without tickets please leave," he said.

"What the fuck are the police doing here anyway?" shouted someone from the back.

"I don't like this," muttered Eva.

"Nor do I," said Avril.

Peake turned to us in the middle of the crowd and said, "I've got something."

We turned to face one another, forming a little circle and Peake drew an envelope out of his jacket pocket and opened it. There were twenty-five amphetamine tablets inside. We took five each and swallowed them. The aftertaste of the speed was the bitterest of all aftertastes. I felt like I'd swallowed a mouthful of salt-water.

The owner in the suit tried to make everyone move back but this had the effect of causing everyone to squeeze forward. The police sergeant politely explained the situation was hopeless. Those without tickets, particularly the man with ginger hair, became angrier.

"You're a fucking pig," the Irishman shouted at him.

A sudden silence fell on the crowd. It was as if there were a collective recognition that some invisible line had been crossed. The sergeant swivelled his head towards the offender.

"Good, you heard, pig, I'm glad you know your name," the Irishman shouted desperately. "I have to put up with your kind in

Belfast and now I come over here and find it's the same decking story."

"That's a breach of the peace," said the sergeant. "I'm going to book you." He handed his clipboard to the club's owner while the policemen beside him drew themselves taller.

"Oh come on, officer," said a very tall, young man at the front of the crowd with Triumph Motorcycles on the back of his jacket. "I don't think it would be the right thing to do," he continued, "and I'm certain the gentleman is very sorry for what he said."

The youth turned towards the mop of red hair from where the abuse had come. "You are sorry, aren't you?" he said.

"I am," said the Irishman so loudly it seemed to me he wasn't in the least contrite.

"All right," said the sergeant, "I'm letting you off with a caution."

He climbed back on to the top step and reclaimed his clipboard.

A sense of relief passed through the crowd.

"Now you're all going to have to follow my instructions," the sergeant continued. "Those without tickets must leave. If you don't leave, I have a squad of men with dogs at the end of the passage and they are going to come and remove you."

No-one moved. For some minutes there was a stalemate with the police urging everyone back and the crowd jostling forward.

The next was inevitable.

"Fucking pig," shouted someone at the sergeant.

The walkie-talkies of the policemen on the steps started crackling and buzzing.

The speed had started to take effect. The bands of muscle in my stomach had begun to ache and although I was in the middle of a crowd, I felt as if I were a long way away from them. There was a great deal of pushing and shoving going on. I didn't feel frightened. I felt as if I were in the sea and all these movements around me were benign, like the swell of the ocean. Then I remembered Eva. I looked around and I couldn't see her. I felt certain she'd fallen down and was being trampled on the ground.

"Eva," I shouted.

There was a lot of noise: whistles going and shouting.

From behind a hand came up and squeezed my shoulder. I half-turned and there was Eva with Avril beside her. "Oh God," she said with something like a smirk on her face.

Then I lost her. The crowd surged forward like a wave, struck something and was sent crashing back.

I stumbled. From my knees I saw around me Doctor Marten boots, ox-blood and cherry coloured, suede-covered stilettos, winklepickers, brothel creepers with grooves running along the thick crêpe soles, monkey boots sporting coloured laces, drainpipe trousers, torn stockings and the hems of skirts.

I thought, I mustn't stay here.

I scrambled to my feet and looked down the passage. From where I stood it seemed to stretch away interminably. The wire mesh gate was thrown back and people were streaming through. The brick walls and the asphalt floor were splashed every few seconds purple and blue from the whirling police lights at the end.

Everyone was running. I was running too. I saw Eva and Avril and Malachy and Peake running. I thought I could hear the chains on the back of Avril's jacket tinkling as she moved. It was not wise to have taken that speed, said a faraway voice.

I was running harder. My lungs hurt and I thought I was going to be sick.

At the end of the alleyway were policemen running towards us. Their truncheons were raised. There were alsatian dogs barking and straining on their leashes. As the mass moved towards us, lit up for an instant of a second at a time, it was like the moment in a discotheque when the stroboscopic light is turned on.

"We're ticket holders," the shout went up ahead and I could see arms outstretched with green tickets which the dogs leapt towards, and as their teeth closed on the skin of wrists or on arms through leather, the screaming really started and the tickets fluttered away, and truncheons fell and there was blood everywhere.

The police kept running forward, moving their truncheons in slow motion. I don't know if I was hit. Probably a glancing blow. Certainly I fell. I could see legs again and the coarse brown fur of a dog, and I could hear quite distinctly its claws scraping on the tarmac. I went to get up but someone held me and the next thing that happened was that two policemen, with their arms locked around mine, were dragging me along and my heels were jiggling as they bounced over the ground. I felt like a half-drowned man being dragged out of the surf.

"But I'm a ticket holder," I shouted and I had it still in my hand, I could feel it, because since Malachy had given each of us our ticket, I hadn't let go of it. They didn't hear me and I tilted my head back and looked up at the grey sky above the alley and wished for it to be clear so I could see the stars.

I was taken off with others in a van. I remember only the way the van seemed to press against my side every time we turned a corner. I began to think the organs inside my chest were being squashed and pushed and forced out of alignment. Then I remembered the others. I looked around but I couldn't see Eva or anyone.

In the police station, I showed a man in a uniform behind a desk my green ticket. I started to explain the situation and I heard him saying, "Have you been drinking?"

We were all put into a room and told we would be processed. It was large with grey walls and neon strips which swung slowly overhead.

I found a clear piece of wall which no-one else was leaning against and kicked away the cigarette butts lying on the floor. The flattened shapes slipped away like stones on ice.

I went as if to sit down when I thought, There'll be ash on the floor from those cigarettes. The idea of getting my trousers dirty was unbearable. I got down on my knees and huffed. Little flecks of ash and pieces of grit fluttered away, reminding me of leaves in the wind. I was mesmerised.

After I was certain the linoleum was clear, I finally sat down. I leant against the wall and closed my eyes. I imagined my breathing was slowing down and my heart was beating less intensely and my lungs were taking in less and less air. Everything was closing down.

Something tapped my shin. I opened my eyes. It was Malachy. He sat down beside me. "I feel terrible," he said. "Not my usual celestial self at all."

It seemed like a wonderful joke and we both started to laugh.

There was no processing and there were no charges. We were simply told after a couple of hours that we could go. Somehow Avril and Eva and Peake had evaded arrest. Of course they couldn't get into the car because Malachy, who was in the police station, had the keys. So they telephoned John. He took a minicab to Willesden, taking with him his spare set, and the three of them drove to the police station. They were waiting for us when we were let out.

We drove home in silence. Peake and Avril were let out at their homes. When we got to the house, I glided after the others into the kitchen. Teresa put a sandwich down in front of me. I lifted off the top slice. There were lettuce leaves, crinkled like the inside of an ear, little drops of water scattered on them here and there. The tomatoes in thin slices held yellow pips like the eyes of a bird. The powdery yolk of an egg had an almost blue sheen to it like a bruise.

I felt a pressing feeling in my bladder. I drifted up to the bathroom and watched my pee, briny and yellow, curving into the bowl. When I finished I flushed the lavatory.

I was waiting for the sound of the cistern refilling, when I noticed several cans of shaving cream on the window ledge. I got one and started squirting out the foam. The lavatory bowl gradually began to fill up with it. When the aerosol was empty I took another and noted with grim satisfaction there were four more to go.

I finally got the shaving cream up to the level of the rim. In my eyes it was a cake I had below me. I found a tube of red toothpaste and iced it lovingly with whirls, squiggles and loops.

I was contemplating my work when I heard a voice from downstairs, "Are you all right up there?" It was Teresa I think calling.

"Just dandy," I shouted back. I flushed and the whole confection disappeared with a slurp, leaving a crease of foam around the rim.

I went back to the kitchen and again Teresa asked, "Are you all right?"

For the rest of the night I lay on my bed. I felt faintly nauseous.

Through my mind churned everything it seemed I had ever said and done but always returning to one event. It was something which had happened before we had left for The Badhouse ...

Crossing the landing on my way down stairs, Eva had called out to me from her bedroom. My spirits lifted, as they always did at the sound of her voice.

I went into her room. Eva was sitting at the large leather-topped table under the window looking out to the front. It was littered with lumps of tailor's chalk, several big pairs of scissors, and patterns cut from brown paper and pinned on to fabric. She was combing her hair.

I stood for a moment listening to the sound of the tines on her scalp. I remembered as a child just the same swishing noise when I had stood behind my mother at her dressing table. Then the thought crept up on me, Reach out and touch her. I imagined the feel of her hair between my fingers would be cool. My mother's hair always was. As my arm started to rise involuntarily, she caught my eye in the fitting mirror standing beside the table. The look which I saw was not of surprise but, I thought, expectation. Then I became self-conscious and I thought, What I'm about to do isn't right. I felt my arm start to drop and within an instant, the permission which I had seen on her face vanished, as quickly as a fish darting away from a shadow.

"No leather jacket?" she asked.

"I haven't got one."

I was wearing a sweat shirt, jeans, and black suede shoes with pointed toes. They were Malachy's. He had given them to me when I had admired them. We were the same foot size.

"Will I look out of place?" I asked.

"I shouldn't think so," she replied and gave one of her big smiles which said, Everything's all right, there's nothing to worry about.

I told her about my day, cutting down an old pear tree in the garden and chopping out the roots. After this, I'd taped up the glass in the greenhouse in preparation to painting the woodwork. I liked doing odd jobs around the place.

"It's so good you turned up," she said suddenly, though this didn't follow on from what I'd been saying. I had found it difficult at first but now I was used to these abrupt changes of course which she took when talking. I liked them if I'm to be honest.

"Ah shucks," I was about to say but I couldn't because she continued, "I always knew you would. I had this sense."

She stood up in that way women do which signals they want to be alone. I left the room ...

I had been over this several dozen, perhaps a hundred times when I noticed the dawn chorus starting. Craning my head back, I saw the first light showing behind the curtain. I had to admit, I wasn't going to get to sleep now.

I'd meant to keep a diary that summer. Well now's the time to start, spoke the same irritating voice which had said it wasn't wise to take the speed.

I got up and went to the table. I had an oilskin-covered notebook I'd bought specially for the purpose.

I'd fallen in love with Eva, and it suddenly occurred to me that a way to disentangle the whole mess might be to write everything down and then keep going for the whole summer.

Once I heard the first scratch of the pen on the paper, I felt the power of the speed in my blood. I knew I could write for hours.

I had to go to the beginning ...

I got off the aeroplane at Heathrow airport. I went down to Immigration and waited. When I got to the head of the queue, I handed over my passport.

"How long are you staying in the country?" the official asked.

"A couple of months. Maybe three."

"Business or pleasure?"

"Pleasure. I have relatives here. I'm hoping to contact them."

"Uh-huh," he said, opening a book. He held the cover up in such a way that I could not see what was listed in it.

Then I heard, "What is the purpose for your wishing to enter the United Kingdom?"

I looked around. At the next lectern along stood a couple, both in their early fifties. On her head the woman wore a straw hat with imitation flowers on her brim. Her dress was black with a white pattern, white lapels and a white belt around her middle. Her husband had a long sad face and wore a jumper with buttons up the front under his check jacket. The official in front of them wore a double-breasted jacket which was too big for his bony frame. His lips were thin and his nose was pointed.

"Why – are – you – coming – to – Britain?" the official shouted at them, falling back on that traditional standby: if they don't speak your language, bellow.

The couple looked frightened and spoke rapidly and quietly between themselves in French.

Finally the husband said, speaking with a very strong French accent, "We have come to see my son."

"What is his address in the UK?"

"Engineering, the University of Keele."

"He's a student?"

"Yes."

"What is his address?"

"Engineering."

"He's at the University of Keele?"

"Yes."

"What's his address?"

"Engineering, with electronics . . ."

The official I was in front of handed back my passport.

"Have you funds?"

I touched the traveller's cheques which were inside my breast pocket.

"May I see?"

He took the rubber band off the bundle and began to leaf through, his lips moving as he counted the notes.

He was very white-skinned with thin black hair which his scalp showed through. It was the grey colour of city snow, just before a thaw. His fingernails were ragged at the ends because they'd been bitten. He was a small man who was made to seem bigger because he sat on a big chair behind a raised lectern. Looking around the hall I saw all the others were just like him. Small men and women perched at a ridiculous height. Their job was to size up all of us foreigners pressing at the gates of their city, and keep as many out as possible.

I turned to look sideways again.

"Under the terms of the Immigration Act of 1974, I do not have leave to allow you entry . . ." boomed the official in the double-breasted jacket.

I looked at the faces of the couple. They did not understand what was being said but they understood the tone.

"*Mon fils,*" said the woman, speaking for the first time. She took an eight by ten photograph out of her handbag and started to weep.

"I'm sorry that's of no use to me whatsoever," said the official.

The photograph showed a young man in a gown and mortar board. Like his parents, he was black.

"Here you are, Mr Harvey. Have a nice trip," I heard the official saying and saw he was handing back the cheques.

I put them in my pocket and hurried off.

* * *

I retrieved my luggage and went out into the arrivals lounge. Somewhere in the middle of the floor I stopped and started thinking. I had a little cash but maybe I should go to the bank and get a little more? I needed some dental floss. Maybe there was a drug store open?

I looked around and then up. In airports it's always up. There was a board covered with signs and arrows. Incomprehensible. The excitement I had felt was now all gone and in its place I felt a sense of anti-climax. I had come all that way. I had arrived. Somewhere in the city was my father and his family. But they weren't there to meet me.

Before coming, I decided not to contact them. Instead I had planned a *fait accompli*. I'd just turn up. It had seemed like a good idea back at home where I'd imagined all sorts of brilliant situations . . . I'd telephone and I'd immediately be summoned to a wonderful dinner. Or I'd go to the street where my father's house was. I'd meet him coming out of it. He'd stop and look at me. "Don't I know you from somewhere?" he'd say. "Your face seems awfully familiar." "I'm Amy's son," I'd reply and at that point the fantasy would end . . .

As I stood in the arrivals lounge, people all around, their shoes scuffing and squeaking on the floor, a woman's voice coming from the public address system, the plan no longer seemed so good. I began to feel a little sorry for myself. I didn't like the idea of finding my way into a strange city. I didn't like the idea of the room in the guest house I had arranged to take. I didn't like the idea that in the evening, far from the way I had pictured it at home, the truth was actually that I would have to go out into a town where I didn't know my way around and find myself something to eat. It would probably be a hamburger.

I went and sat down on a plastic seat and smoked a cigarette. In front of me there was a shop, its windows lined with transparent legs with different coloured stockings stretched over them. I stared at these legs for a long time.

Then I got up and went down the hall. I bought an orange juice from a fruit bar. The counterhand wore a straw boater and said, "Have a nice day." The drink had the bitter taste of peel, which I don't like but I finished it anyway. Then I caught my first underground train into London.

It was a long ride in a clattering, swaying train. I looked out the dirty window at the suburbs of the city spreading below. Every sight, sound and smell was new. My spirits began to rise again.

Mother's name is Amy Harvey. She calls herself a "war baby". She was born the day the Japanese struck at Pearl Harbor in 1941. She grew up on a farm in New Hampshire. After she left school she went to Manchester, the biggest city in the state. She worked as a typist in a small insurance company and met her first husband, John Michael O'Neill. They married in 1960 on her nineteenth birthday. They stayed together about a year and a half. They divorced and she married a man she had known from childhood. Hudson Harvey's parents were friends of her parents. With her new husband, she moved to New Jersey. He worked – he still does – in New York. I was the first-born of the family. Two more followed. My mother kept the letters which John Michael O'Neill wrote her when they were courting, on top of her wardrobe in an old suitcase with a broken handle. Sometimes as children we would get them down, puzzle at the spidery, sloping writing and laugh at words like "dearest", "darling" and "love". Her first husband was not a secret from us.

When Annie was born I was six. I remember in the months after the birth, Mum and Dad would often argue. The rows were long and loud and often public. They also both drank a great deal. Sometimes my father Hudson would not come home for the night. During one argument, which I have never forgotten, he pointed his finger at me and said, "I don't want any cuckoos in the nest." I didn't understand this. Nor did I follow what was happening an hour or so later, when he came and found me and said he was sorry. He took me out to an ice-cream parlour and let me eat as much as I wanted. "We get along great, don't we?" I remember him saying over and over again. At some point, which I don't remember, the arguments ended. My parents stayed

together. Annie took me to be her brother and my father stopped
worrying about the cuckoo in the nest.

One evening, a couple of years ago, I blithely said to my
mother, "How come I don't look like Patsy or Annie? They're
blonde, they're brown eyed, they look like you and father put
together. But I have black hair. I have blue eyes. I don't look like
anyone else in the family."

"You're your father's child," she said. "Don't make any
mistake about it."

It sounded like a lie. I started asking questions. Some months
later the answer came to me from nowhere and I said to her,
"Your first husband is my father, isn't he?" "Yes," she said, "he
is."

She met John Michael O'Neill in the late fifties. He was an
illegal immigrant working in a factory making electrical compo-
nents. He married my mother to legitimise his position. They
were both under twenty. Within a few months of marrying, he
started seeing another girl. Hardly surprising really given his age.
The girl was also an illegal immigrant, also from Ireland. My
mother, for which she is still ashamed, reported this girl to the
authorities. The girl was deported. It was the end of the marriage
and my father left America. Hudson immediately asked Amy to
marry him. She agreed. A few weeks after the engagement she
then discovered she was pregnant by John Michael O'Neill. She
hadn't noticed before with everything that had been happening.
Hudson said it didn't matter. Not to him anyway. They went
through the ceremony and not long after I was born. Six years
later, Annie came along, there was the bumpy patch when my
father presumably felt jealous of my presence, and they decided
to tell John Michael O'Neill about me. I understand it was my
father's suggestion. He thought it was the right thing to do. He
believed a man should know who his children were.

My mother had no idea where my father was. They hadn't
been in touch for six years. She wrote to him care of the Post
Office in the village of Donegal where he came from. The letter
was forwarded. Eventually my father wrote back. He was married
again, with children. My mother kept this letter separate from the
courting letters in the battered suitcase on top of her wardrobe.

She only showed it to me last year. "I'm glad to know what I anyway suspected," he wrote. "I understand you haven't told him (and I also understand why you haven't) but if the situation ever changes, I'd be happy to see him. I've discussed this at home and my wife Teresa would be as happy to see him as I am."

I started asking my mother about him. She said she didn't remember much. His village was called Glendowan. I had his skin colouring, his blue eyes and his build.

I decided I must go to London to see my other family but that I was not going to write in advance to let them know I was coming. My father had said he'd be happy to see me, I reasoned, because he knew Amy hadn't told me. It's easy making promises knowing you may not have to keep them.

I planned to come to London for a summer. I worked and I saved. Not until I was on the aeroplane did I begin to worry about my plan. What would happen if the O'Neills were away for the summer themselves? I'd end up being in London for three whole months without being able to do what I'd gone there to do. I quickly drank three free Bloody Marys and stopped worrying. I said to myself, Well, if they're not there you have friends and friends of friends to contact, and if the worst comes to the very worst, you can always get on an aeroplane and go back home.

From Heathrow I went directly to the Cumberland Hotel in Ebury street, where I had arranged to stay. It was an old building, with a notice hanging in the front window which read, *Vacancies*.

The room was at the back. There was a single bed, a handbasin and a chest of drawers. It smelt vaguely of gas. The window overlooked a paved yard.

I had the address of my father but no telephone number. I went down to the desk. It was at the far end of the hall. The ceiling above and the walls on either side were covered with mirrored glass. The young girl on duty was studying the hem of her skirt at the back by looking over her shoulder into the mirror.

I gave her the address written on the piece of paper and she gave me a telephone directory for the letters E to K. I turned to O'Neill and there he was, O'Neill, J. M., 36, Dyson avenue, Hampton Wick. I wrote down the telephone number and went upstairs.

In my room I lit a cigarette. I wondered why I wasn't feeling extraordinary. This was a momentous occasion.

I picked up the receiver which smelt vaguely of perspiration, and started to read the instructions on the laminated sheet on the bedside bureau. I was reading for such a long time, the tone stopped and a high-pitched whining started. I put the receiver down. I felt no sense that a special moment had arrived. I could have been about to telephone anyone.

I picked up the receiver again. I dialled 9. There was a clicking noise as the connection to the outside line was made. I dialled the number carefully. The telephone rang at the other end three or four times. It was picked up.

"Hello," said a woman's voice, "who is it?"

I gave my name and asked for Mr O'Neill.

"Hello," she said, as if she knew me. "He's at work but we've been expecting you." She had a strong foreign accent.

What had happened of course was the one thing that hadn't crossed my mind. My mother had written, in advance, to warn them of my coming. We arranged to meet the next day which was Sunday.

It was now the late afternoon. I bought a map at a stationer's on a corner in Ebury street and walked to St James's park. I rented a deck chair. The chestnut trees, the office workers streaming through the park after work, the men emptying the trash cans, and everything else I saw sent shivers of excitement through me. I'd never seen any of this before.

Then there was tomorrow but I didn't think about it. I wouldn't let myself. It was like a present, wrapped and waiting to be opened.

By the following morning, however, my feelings felt anaesthetised. I was not simply calm but in a sense under absolute control. Some wise unknown part of my personality had decided not to let me be excited. I suppose this was a defence mechanism.

I went to Waterloo as instructed. The timetables were in the middle of the concourse, pinned up behind glass. An old man was studying one of them. I watched him remove his false teeth. The gumshield was a lurid purple colour. He wrapped the set in his handkerchief and put them in his pocket. Then he wrote something down in a notebook and walked off.

I found my train and went to the platform. The train had not arrived. The stones between the tracks were greasy and littered with rubbish. I noticed cigarette butts scrumpled up, two straws, an empty book of matches, ring pulls, the wrapping from a pair of Honeymoon tights, and a McDonald's styrofoam pack with something in it, which two grey pigeons were trying to peck open. In the distance I saw the man with the false teeth. The mouth of the station and a grey sky were behind him.

I went up to him and saw he was holding his notebook open.

"Hello," I said.

At home I doubt I'd have done this but here it didn't occur to me he might find it odd to be addressed by a stranger.

"What are you doing?" I continued.

"Spotting."

The pages of the notebook were covered with columns of handwritten numbers. He lifted the binoculars hanging around his neck to his eyes and followed the train which had just appeared. It glided into the station two or three platforms away. There was a screeching sound of brakes. He dropped the binoculars and wrote another figure at the bottom of one of the columns.

"Train spotting," he said and turned towards me. His false teeth were back in again. He had very short grey hair and wide staring blue eyes.

"You write down the numbers of trains?"

"Every Sunday. Since I was a boy. I've got eighty-five notebooks." He waved the one he was holding.

"I've made a note of a lot of the trains in this country and probably most of the trains in the south-east and round London. It's an important historical record. I shall write about it soon."

His name was Mr Shrotton. I asked what started him?

"It's in the genes. Dad was a signal man. Down at Merton. Spent all my boyhood in the box with him, watching the trains. He wasn't meant to but he used to let the spotters into his box, especially if the weather came bad. Not many boxes now, which is a great shame."

"What are you going to write about?"

"I don't know. You meet a lot of people when you do this. A lot of characters. I think that's what I'll concentrate on and sort of keep the trains in the background. Then again I might die tomorrow and that would be that."

My train came. It was painted blue and white and the doors opened at the touch of a button. I got on and found a seat. When we started to shunt off I looked for Mr Shrotton. I wanted to wave goodbye but he had gone.

I got out of the train at Hampton Wick and found my way to Dyson avenue. It was a short road lined with cherry trees. It was June and the blossom had already come and gone. The tree bark was a peculiar plum colour. I passed an Edwardian villa where a man sat playing the piano in the front room. Next door stood a modern bungalow with a gleaming roof. Bright red and yellow marigolds grew in straight lines along the immaculate flowerbeds, and in the drive was a large powerboat sitting on a trailer covered with a tarpaulin. All the other houses stood alone with gardens back and front. I could hear the distant sound of a tolling church bell and the whisper of a garden sprinkler turning. The rain which had spotted the window of the train was gone. It was now a humid, muggy day.

Dyson avenue is a cul-de-sac and the O'Neills lived at the end in number seven. It was a dark brick house with wooden gables painted yellow. I walked down the tile path, passing under the monkey-puzzle tree with its dangling tail-like foliage and pressed the bell. I waited, staring at the inset panes of glass, listening for the sound of footfalls beyond.

A few moments later I got a slight start when I heard a voice saying, "We're in the garden. It's this way."

I turned and saw a girl had put her head around the corner of the house. She wore a man's shirt and its flap hung down at the back. Her legs were bare.

I followed her down the passage by the side of the house. There were dustbins with "O'Neill" painted on them, a coal bunker and a slime-covered ladder padlocked to the wall.

We emerged at the end on to a patio paved with square yellow stones and a barbecue at the side, its hearth filled with ash. A veranda ran along the back of the house, a ping-pong table with a tightly stretched net looming inside, while silvery kitchen taps gleamed in a kitchen behind. We skirted a bed of shrubs with yellow flowers and came round into the garden.

It was big and square. Birds were singing and there was the smell of earth. In the middle of the lawn sat a man; a woman about the same age as he was; and a younger man.

The man got up from the garden chair and came towards me. He was wearing shorts and a pair of flip flops. He shook my hand. This was my father, John Michael O'Neill.

He introduced me first to his wife. My step-mother Teresa was a woman in her late forties with black hair. Then to the girl who had come to fetch me. My half-sister Eva had taken off her shirt and was wearing a swimming costume underneath. She had red hair and blue eyes and I immediately felt attracted to her. Finally, he introduced me to my half-brother who was sitting on a swinging seat with a shade overhead.

"Malachy, this is Malachy," said my father.

I'd known in advance I was going to be embarrassed by this moment, and I was. I felt all the colour leaving my face.

"We're having a drink," my father continued, sounding as if he couldn't imagine I should be surprised that he had two sons with the same name.

I said, "Why not?"

Teresa handed me a glass. "There we are." It was cold and smelt of mint.

The aluminium chair creaked when I sat down and it tilted slightly sideways because the lawn was uneven. I nearly spilt my drink.

I wanted to say something but I could not think of what. I had the feeling a silence was about to descend, just the same as when people are eating together who don't know one another very well, and the conversation dries up and suddenly the only sound is the one of knives and forks scraping on plates. I hate those moments. I can't think of anything to say and this was another of them. Sitting in the garden I could feel a flush starting. It began at the neck and moved up the chin to the face.

"Did you find you way easily?"

Thank God, I thought.

It was Eva who had spoken. She was sitting on the swinging seat, painting her large toe-nail red. I could smell the varnish, half-astringent, half-alcohol.

"I had no trouble."

I put the glass to my lips and tried to swallow a larger mouthful than I should have taken. A small dribble ran down my chin.

"Here." Teresa passed a paper napkin to me.

"Are you from Germany?" I heard myself asking. Teresa sounded to my ears as though she came from there.

"Have a guess," said Malachy from beside his sister. The bottle of varnish was on the seat between them and her toe-nails were vividly red against the grass.

"I don't know," I said.

"It's not very important," said Teresa, turning towards her son, "and anyway how can he tell?"

Eva looked at me and mouthed the name of the country but without forming a sound. I couldn't understand. She repeated this. ". . ."

"Germany," I said, "no, I've said that."

". . ." mouthed Eva.

"Poland."

Eva shook her head. ". . ."

I tried to understand what she meant but couldn't.

"Czechoslovakia." It was the next country I could think of.

"No," said my namesake.

"Malachy, I don't think we need to go on with this game any longer," said Teresa. "It's very rude to put a guest through this kind of ordeal."

". . .," Eva repeated cryptically.

I thought, I'm just going to have to work my way through all the countries of middle Europe until I get to hers.

"Yugoslavia," I said.

"No," Malachy replied loudly. "Hungary." He started to laugh and threw himself back in the swinging seat.

"Malachy, look what you've done," Eva cried.

Throwing himself back, Malachy had tipped the bottle of varnish off the seat. It was lying on its side on the lawn, and it had been for long enough for most of the red nail polish inside it to trickle out and cover several blades of grass.

"When did you come to London?" my father asked.

"Last Thursday."

"You flew?"

"Yes."

Eva took a page from the Business section of one of the newspapers and laid it over the spilt varnish. It soaked in, like blood.

"Free drinks?"

"Yes."

"How many did you have?"

"I don't remember," I said, although I did.

"Do you remember that time going out to Crete?" said John turning to his wife.

Teresa sat on the garden chair opposite me, her thighs lying side by side and her feet flat on the ground. She wore a khaki-coloured dress belted around the middle.

"You made a disgrace of yourself Dad," said Eva.

He turned back towards me.

"Free booze. Whatever you wanted. I started on gin, moved on to wine, and finished with brandy. It was a three-hour flight and by the time we arrived, I was gone. I've never known to this day how I got from the airport to the hotel."

"We were with you Dad," said Malachy. "Your family, we carried you."

"I had a complete blackout," continued John, looking directly at me. "I was on a plane and the next thing I knew I woke up in a hotel bedroom."

"I-don't-remember-nothing," slurred Eva like a drunk.

"And where are you staying?" It was Teresa who spoke.

"Near Victoria Station."

"I did some work around there once. Somewhere in Pimlico," said John.

Teresa stretched her legs out and crossed one ankle over the other. She swirled the ice inside her glass and stared at me.

"Are you staying in a hotel?" she asked.

"It calls itself a hotel but it's what you call a guest house."

"Very expensive I would imagine," said my father. "London's become very expensive."

"I don't know."

"You haven't had your bill yet," he said and chuckled.

I could sense my half-brother, listening to everything being said although he was reading the newspaper. Beads of perspiration had formed on my upper lip. I wiped them away.

"Your mother said you were coming to England for a good long time," said Teresa.

"For the summer, yes."

"I hope we're going to see lots of you."

"I hope so."

Eva's right leg was bent and the heel of her foot rested against her sex. She ran the brush around the inside of the bottle to get out whatever varnish was inside. On her thigh there was a birthmark. It was a squashed shape, the colour of rhubarb. I stared at it for a moment and then feeling my face reddening, it had suddenly occurred to me someone might have noticed I was staring, I lifted my eyes to the bottom of the garden. There were apple trees covered with lichen, the same green as copper when it corrodes, and a sad-looking greenhouse, the paintwork peeling and shadows of green slime covering some of the panes.

"What do you do?" Teresa asked. She was leaning forward and smiling.

"I'm going to be a student. At the end of the summer, I mean. Up until now I've been working. For the housing department of the state government in New Jersey."

"How old are you?"

"Twenty-five."

"It's a very good age to start higher education," said Teresa. "Much better than rushing on from school into it."

"It's my twenty-fifth any minute now," said Malachy from behind his newspaper.

The same name and shortly the same age.

"When I was a young lad there wasn't such a thing as a university on our side of the tracks," said John.

"Oh Dad," said Eva and gave a little mock groan.

"What are you going to study?" asked my half-brother.

"Literature or history. I don't have to make up my mind for a year or two."

I shyly added something about wanting to be a writer. None of them responded and that was the end of the conversation.

The clouds above had moved away and now there was a blue sky overhead. I felt the warmth of the sun on my face and because of the sudden brightness I had to squint. A petal, from one of the roses in the flowerbed to the side, fell away from its head. It was so still the noise as it landed on the ground could be clearly heard. It was like a tiny little sigh.

"Whoopee, the sun," said Eva standing up and stretching her arms into the air. She had the same slight build as her mother. "I'm going to sunbathe."

"Before you do, will you refill our glasses?" her mother asked.

As Eva walked towards me I had a good look at her. Her red hair came down to her shoulders. Her eyes were a pale colour of blue. The most prominent feature was her wide mouth. She took my glass.

"And how's your mam?" asked John suddenly. He had his head tilted to the side and brushed away the grey hair which had fallen over one eye.

For a moment I didn't feel anything and then I felt completely dumbfounded by the question. It was not possible to answer it straight off like I had all the others.

"Pretty good," was all I was finally able to manage.

"Give her our good wishes, won't you?" Teresa said brightly.

"Oh yes," I said, wondering what exactly she meant? That I would get off the aeroplane in New Jersey, go straight home and say, "John and the second Mrs O'Neill send greetings"? My

mother was a good woman. She had written and told the
O'Neills I was coming. But I knew when I got back home, she
would be wondering if I now loved her a little less than before? If
I had transferred my affections in some part to my new family? If
perhaps I even blamed her a little for the fact that I didn't grow
up with my real father? Good wishes from her first husband's
wife would be almost one of the last things I would communicate.
I might not even convey them at all.

Eva handed back my glass. Pieces of fruit floated in the drink.

"Call me when it's lunch or if you want a hand," she said to
her mother. She started to walk towards the end of the garden.

"Have you ever been to Manchester, New Hampshire?" asked
John.

"No."

"I wonder if it's changed? It was quite a rough town in my
day. I suppose it isn't any more."

"I don't think he knows. He hasn't been there," said Teresa.

"Just asking," said her husband.

At the bottom of the garden, screened by the apple trees, was a
reclining canvas seat. Eva, sitting on the edge with her back to us,
was pulling down her swim suit.

"You are staying for lunch, aren't you?" Teresa asked.

"Yes," I replied.

Eva threw her swim suit on the ground and lay back. Only her
two brown feet showed and the colour supplement which she
had brought with her to read.

"Do you like salmon?"

"Great."

"I'm so pleased," said Teresa.

John and Teresa

From America, John made his way by ship to Southampton. He took a train to Liverpool, intending there to catch the ferry to Dun Loaghaire. He was going to have a week home in Ireland. Then at Crewe he had a change of heart. He remembered his uncle in Northampton. He swopped trains and got into the dreary Midlands town about three o'clock.

His uncle was his father's younger brother – Patrick O'Neill. The only address which his uncle had ever given at the top of any of his letters was the Battle of Jutland public house.

John asked the ticket collector at the station if he knew where the Battle of Jutland was. Of course he didn't. Northampton was a city with dozens of pubs. At the post office, however, he made more progress. He found the Battle of Jutland in the telephone directory. A counter clerk drew him a map and gave him instructions how to get there.

He caught a bus to the city's outskirts and started to walk. It was a district of low, redbrick houses, row after row of them. On some of the terrace ends there were grocer shops or little off-licences. There were almost no cars in the streets and most of the street lamps were bent from children swinging off them from pieces of rope. Finally, he found it. The Battle of Jutland was a detached building clad with mock-Tudor beams. The sign was a naive illustration of a Dreadnought ploughing through a rough sea. It was about five o'clock and the pub was shut.

He went round to the side and banged on a likely looking door. A dog barked inside and the publican appeared. He was carrying a Staffordshire bull terrier in his arms.

The publican had never heard of Patrick O'Neill. "But that

doesn't mean he doesn't come to the Battle of Jutland," he added. Many Irishmen drank there and several were called Patrick. John asked if he could wait inside and was told that was out of the question. The licensing laws stipulated no public on the premises until 5.30.

It was February and very cold. He walked up and down the street briskly and bought himself a portion of chips from a chipper. At 5.29 he was outside the Battle of Jutland with a couple of other men and heard the sound of the bolts banging back inside.

The public bar had ochre walls and wooden tables and benches. He bought a pint of bitter and sat by the hearth. There were charred pieces of newspaper and half-burnt lumps of coal in the grate. He was beginning to think he had made a mistake when half-a-dozen men in filthy clothes trooped into the bar. One of them was his uncle.

Patrick O'Neill was a contractor, specialising in the laying of asphalt and tarmacadam. He sat down at a table, took several hundred pounds out of his pocket which he counted into piles, and began to pay the men he had come in with and others who followed.

This was Friday evening. On Monday morning my father started working for his uncle, helping to lay down the tarmacadam at the back of a new shopping mall in Coventry.

It was 1961. Public spending by local authorities was high. The slums, and those parts of the cities which had been bombed in the war, were being cleared away and new buildings were being put up. John worked the Midlands with his uncle and the gang, from Nottingham in the north to Luton in the south, tarmacadaming roads, playgrounds, car parks and housing estates.

Five years earlier, the woman who was to become his second wife left Hungary, immediately after the 1956 revolution. She was fourteen years old when she arrived in the refugee camp in Vienna.

Teresa's mother had studied English for a while and had passed on some knowledge of the language to her daughter. For this reason Teresa decided she wanted to go into exile in an English speaking country. When she applied, Canada and Australia were gone but the British quota still wasn't used up, and so she was sent to England.

When she arrived, Teresa was placed with an old Hungarian doctor and his wife, refugees from earlier troubles – from Béla Kún's regime of the early twenties. The doctor and his wife lived near the Midlands town of Northampton. Teresa spoke Hungarian at home but learnt good English too, although she spoke it with a strong accent. She always maintained later too many familiar sounds at home were to blame.

The old doctor died, and then his wife within a few months of him. Teresa found a job in the Northampton hospital as a cleaner. Soon she rose to become a cook. She had ambitions to train as a nurse.

She was twenty when she and John first set eyes on one another. It was a Sunday morning in a Northampton parish church. John was sitting in a pew on the aisle side, idly glancing back over his shoulder every now and then to see who was coming in, when she saw him and he saw her.

What he saw was a small woman with a well-proportioned figure and, like her daughter Eva, with a head which seemed a little too large for the rest of her body. This was attractive. She had blondish hair which she wore under a beret, and blue eyes and a wide mouth. Her coat was open and underneath she wore a grey woollen dress with a white collar.

When she saw John for that first time, he was a year older than her. He was wearing a dark suit and a tie. At that moment they both felt overwhelmed by something.

She walked past him and went and sat down at the aisle end of a pew, three or four rows in front. John stared at her neck and her ears throughout the service. Twice when the congregation were standing and singing, she looked back at him.

Just before the end of the service he undid his shoelaces. When the moment came to lead out, he suddenly exclaimed loudly and lifted his right foot on to the seat. Never was a lace tied so carefully and he repeated this on the other foot. By this time Teresa was level with him. He stepped out into the throng of people and, keeping his eye on her beret, followed her out.

At the foot of the steps outside stood a trestle table with newspapers laid out on it. As soon as she saw them, Teresa had an inspiration. She stopped and asked the news vendor, speaking with an exaggerated accent in order to slow up communication, if he had Hungarian newspapers?

The vendor made the pretence of leafing through piles of the *Kerryman*, the *Clare Champion* and the *Sunday Independent* among others, and then said no, he didn't have what she wanted. This gave John the time he needed to catch up with her. He was oblivious to the fact that actually this was her intention. Coming in on the end of the conversation he saw his chance. There were only provincial or national Irish newspapers on sale, he explained. Not even English newspapers. This was because all the congregation were Irish.

What was said next, neither can remember. Someone said something. The other replied. It happens so often doesn't it? The before and after remain but the key moment is lost.

What I know – they have both told me about this – is John walked with her into the centre of the city. He thought about inviting her into a public house but he decided that might be a mistake. He asked instead if she would like a cup of tea in the railway station buffet. Teresa in fact wanted a drink but said nothing. She didn't want to create an unfavourable impression either.

He walked her later to the hospital where she started work at midday and he was there to meet her in the evening, when the shift finished, with a bunch of roses wrapped in newspaper. He had meant to go home to Glendowan in Donegal for a week's summer holiday but he stayed in Northampton so he could see Teresa every day.

They started courting. John told her he'd been married and was divorced. He would probably not have done this if she had been Irish. Because she was a foreigner, she provoked none of the reflexes which would have been inevitable with one of his own race.

They married, within six weeks of their meeting, in August 1962. The ceremony was performed at the side altar in the church where they had first seen one another. Teresa's family were all in

Hungary and Patrick O'Neill had to give her away. A landau pulled by a chestnut bay – popular at the time at Irish weddings in Northampton – conveyed them from the church to the Derryowen. John had done the tarmacadaming work at this newly built Irish social club, and had been happy to accept the slightly reduced rates they had offered.

The reception was in what was called the Shannon hall (as distinct from the Foyle rooms or the Liffey bar which completed the watery metaphor). It was decorated with buntings and balloons and a huge banner, Welcome Mr & Mrs O'Neill. It still smelt of concrete and new paint.

Teresa was offered the use of the Manager's office. She went there to re-apply her make-up and spent ten solitary minutes sitting at the desk in the bare room and weeping. It was partly the loneliness of marrying without the presence of her family. Even her mother would have pleased her, she thought, as salty tears ran down her cheeks. Because of her father's position, neither he nor his wife were granted a passport when they applied to travel abroad to the wedding. As well as their absence there was also the horse. Teresa was allergic to the dust from these animals. John's two elder sisters, Maureen and Kathleen, – they had come over from Donegal for the wedding – eventually came to find her. When they came into the room they both saw Teresa had been crying but pretended not to have noticed.

The guests were given a punch made from cider and brandy and invited to sit at the trestle tables. They were served cold chicken on hot plates. With each portion came an uncut tomato, cucumber slices, pickled onions, a beetroot and green lettuce. Each piece of salad was on a separate part of the plate. Later there was a three-tiered cake which Teresa had to cut while making a wish with the knife held upside-down, a speech from Father McBride who had performed the ceremony, and half a glass of warm champagne for everyone with which to drink the health of the bride and groom. Then the tables were cleared away, the bottles of whisky came out, and a ceilidh band started to play on the small stage. Teresa was enthusiastic about The Siege of Limerick, the Kerry Pipers and the other set dances. She performed an elegant waltz with Patrick O'Neill and a fast foxtrot with Father McBride. Several women commented on how well she was bearing up, considering she had no family present. John O'Neill's sisters did not say what they had seen.

For their honeymoon, the couple went to a small hotel in Wells-next-the-sea in north Norfolk. Teresa used the cap. In her country, she told John, many Catholics did and no-one minded, and because she was a stranger he accepted this. It was true, what she had said, as far as it went. Before she'd left Budapest, Teresa had known from eavesdropping and from talking to her mother something about the device (which was fairly widely used), but she hadn't actually come away with one (which her husband could have assumed from what she'd said). What actually had happened was this. The day before her seventeenth birthday, the doctor with whom she'd lodged, had taken her aside. He knew she would have to look after herself one day, so he provided her with a cap and explained to her how to use it. And she had. Teresa lost her virginity to the son of a neighbour, a couple of months before the doctor's death. John either didn't notice or didn't care and the matter was never discussed.

They returned to Northampton. He had rented a small house near the centre of town. When she cooked in the tiny kitchen, all the windows misted over with condensation. It was Teresa's principal memory of those first weeks.

Malachy, conceived in the autumn, was born in May, 1963, six months after the birth of his brother on the other side of the Atlantic. Eva was conceived at Christmas two years later and was born at the end of August in 1966, a fortnight after her parents' wedding anniversary.

If Teresa had stayed in Hungary she would certainly have gone on to university. Her mother was a laboratory technician, her father a printer. She read novels and liked table wine. Her husband, on the other hand, was the son of a Donegal farmer who'd reduced his holding because of drink to a few acres of miserable land. John left school at fourteen; he went to America at eighteen; all his working life in England he'd been in the construction industry. She set about educating him.

She made him read a little and introduced him to the theatre. She made him take an interest in his appearance and his conversation. She began to criticise Catholicism for inventing hell just to frighten people, for being dogmatic and inflexible, and for making claims of infallibility. None the less they went on going to mass. The cap was never mentioned.

Two children, and then Teresa started to study to become a ledger clerk. The tarmacadaming business prospered. John became a director, equal to his uncle. He gave up his foreman's overalls and put on a suit and went down to London to find contracts. Teresa followed with the children. They lived in Raynes Park, a gloomy suburb beyond the end of the Northern Line.

When Eva started school, Teresa went back to work full time. She found a post in the accounts department of Merton council. She started gymnastics again. This had been her greatest passion in Hungary. The instructress introduced her to naturism. With the first serious money that he earned, she made John buy the house in Hampton Wick.

Just before the end of the seventies, John recognised that change was imminent. High spending by local authorities was on the way out, certainly in London and the south. Enterprise was in. He sold his part of the tarmacadaming business back to his uncle, and invested his money. He bought a bakery business in Shepherd's Bush, a third share of a small scaffolding contractor's, and a shoe repairer's in the concourse of the Arndale shopping centre in Wandsworth. He also put money into a pool room in the basement of an Irish dance hall.

Malachy started school at a convent which took boys up to the age of seven, then went to a Catholic primary school, and then to a Catholic comprehensive school. Eva stayed at the convent and went on to Sixth Form college.

Both children made their first Holy Communion at the age of ten. After this, Teresa stopped going to church altogether. Her children followed suit during their adolescence. John stayed with the church but went infrequently.

When he left school, Malachy went to work with his uncle in Northampton to learn the tarmacadaming business. He left after three years and went to Art school to study fine art. His half-brother came the summer of his first year. He was on holiday and working for a butcher, driving carcasses of meat around London. His sister Eva was twenty. She was about to start a course in fashion. She was working temporarily in a chemist's shop.

Diary, Hampton Wick

My second Sunday . . .

In the lobby of the Cumberland Hotel, I began to sign some traveller's cheques. Above and on all sides I was surrounded by mirrors.

To oversee the operation, the girl who was usually behind the desk had fetched the owner. This woman was in her middle forties and the spaces between her front teeth were stained with nicotine.

The owner smoked as she watched me signing. At some point I looked up. A cloud of smoke drifted across. I saw my reflection stretching away to infinity. I felt as if we were all on stage in a conjuring trick. I went back to signing cheques. My hand felt tired and the thought vanished.

I got to Waterloo station with my luggage. I was early. I bought myself a cup of coffee and went and found a place to sit. It was a plastic slat which folded down. Before long I was sliding off it. I sat back and almost immediately this happened again.

On the other side of the station concourse, three men in dirty clothes were sprawled on filthy squares of cardboard. They were ineffectually calling out to passersby and waving bottles. It would have been impossible for one of them to rest where I was, which was presumably the intention. By this means the derelicts were kept to the floor and we, the paying passengers, were undisturbed. I remembered the couple at the airport. If that was what they did to foreigners, it was hardly surprising they did this to their own, I thought.

The train left from the same platform as before. After I had gone through the ticket barrier, I walked down to the end to see if the train spotter was there.

He wasn't anywhere in sight, of course. I felt disappointed. It is always easier to tell strangers about these things. "I'm in love," I wanted to tell him. I might have told the girl behind the desk at the Cumberland Hotel but when the owner had appeared, that had put an end to that.

The train pulled out of the station. We rattled past grimy warehouses, drab office blocks, and came to the first station. It looked abandoned with its cracked platform and weeds growing prolifically but it wasn't because everywhere were new, brightly painted signs reading *Clapham Junction*. Rather than the hard work of cleaning the place up, it was the cheap way of creating a good impression which had been used. "Like an old whore" was the graffiti scrawled on a wall, which seemed about right.

Further down the line, we stopped between stations. Beyond the window, rows and rows of redbrick terraced houses spread along the side of a hill. The wind blew, the carriage shook and spots of rain spattered against the glass. In the street below, the skirts of two women flapped and they struggled to hold them down.

When I came out of the station at Hampton Wick, a fine grey drizzle was falling. The tarmac in the road was glistening. I lifted my holdall onto my shoulder and took the small bags in the other hand. In Dyson avenue, the cherry trees looked as if they'd been dusted with little drops of water. A woman stood waiting while her poodle squatted in the gutter. The wet had got on to my collar. There was a mouldy smell which reminded me of fungus.

I pressed the O'Neills' bell and waited. I noticed the panes of glass in the front door were etched with pictures of camels and palm trees. Behind these a dark moving shadow appeared. I expected the door to be thrown back but instead I found myself looking at a gap of just four inches. In the narrow space between was the face of Teresa. Her hand was at her neck, holding the dressing gown she was wearing tightly closed.

I was starting to wonder if she was ill and if I had got her out of bed, when she threw back the door and said,

"Of course, I'd forgotten. Come in. The others are out for the afternoon. It's just me at home."

I stepped across the threshold and followed her down the

hallway. On the right were the stairs, with pictures on the wall beside it. The door of the living room was on my left. I could hear the sound of people talking inside and the tinkling sound of cutlery against porcelain.

"I'm a naturist," she said, "and some of us are having a tea party. It completely slipped my mind that you were coming, otherwise I'd have made certain my husband or one of the children was here to let you in. They've gone to the park together."

She was ahead of me reaching forward to shut the living room door. I just caught a glimpse of a mixed party of half-a-dozen inside, white and naked, with teacups balanced on their laps.

I climbed the stairs. On the first landing I couldn't help noticing, through an open bedroom door, the clothes of the guests piled onto a bed.

I climbed to the next floor where the ceilings were sloping and there were painted wooden beams.

"It was Eva's when she was younger," said Teresa. "Do you mind if I leave you? I must return to my guests."

She went down the stairs again and I went in. There was a bed with a white cover, some empty shelves and a lamp with its base made from a Mateus Rosé bottle. The window with its diamond-shaped leads was in a box which jutted out from the roof and there was a table in the recess below. I looked down into the garden. The sun had begun to shine palely and, from the apple trees at the bottom, shadows reached out across the grass. Nearby, someone was using a lawnmower with a motor.

My half-brother, Teresa had told me, had his bedroom next door. I went to have a look. It was larger than my room. On the crowded shelves, along with books and boxes of crayons and paints, there were two or three dozen statues of the Virgin Mary, scenes in glass bubbles which filled with snow when agitated, two small steam engines and an enormous collection of model plastic animals. There was also an electric train set laid out on the floor, a doll's house modelled on a modern Irish bungalow in the corner, and many canvasses stored with their faces to the wall. On the old leather armchair below the window lay a book, pages face down and its name on the front, *A Happy Death*.

I went back to my room. I unpacked my clothes into the
wardrobe and the chest of drawers. Four guests from the tea party
ventured into the veranda below. Their bodies through the glass
roof were like big white smears as they faced one another across
the green oblong of the ping-pong table.

I went and lay down on my bed and thought about how lucky
I was to have been invited to stay. Soon after, with the sound of
laughter drifting from below and the hypnotic clack-clack of the
ball as it passed backwards and forwards over the net, I fell asleep.
I dreamt of a naked female torso which was a face; the nipples
were eyes; the belly button was the nose; the sex was the
enormous mouth.

Malachy woke me up.

"It's all clear. You can come downstairs," he said. "The nudists
have gone."

He was by the table under the window. He picked up the
oilskin-covered notebook lying there and started flipping through
the pages.

"Summer diary?" he asked but not sounding offensive as he
easily might have.

I saw a flurry of blue lines on blank pages, like a reproach.

He left and I went downstairs to Eva's room. She was lying on
the bed inside. She was wearing a paisley dress with a cummerbund. I went up to the threshold but I didn't go in.

Hers was a square room with the monkey-puzzle tree outside
the window. The bed was old and large, with a white coverlet on
it. In front of the window was a battered old table with a green
leather top and an old-fashioned office chair which could tip
back. Pictures of her mother and father, and an old enamelled
map of Ireland made by Firestone tyres, hung on the wall.

"How are you?" I asked Eva.

I wanted to hear her trembling voice but she didn't say a word.
She looked at me for several seconds and then turned her face and
buried it in the pillow.

I drifted down to the sitting room where the naturists had taken
tea. It was another big, square space. There was a ceiling rose which
reminded me of a table doily, and a tiled fireplace with tulips in
relief. The geraniums in the corner gave off a strong, chalky smell.

I turned on the television. The programme had something to do with Christianity and social responsibility. At some point Eva slunk in, silent because she was in her stockinged feet. She sat down on the sofa and brought her knees up to her chest under her dress. The cummerbund was gone.

"Are you cold?" I asked.

She shook her head and peered at the screen. The picture showing was of the British Prime Minister. She had been re-elected just before I arrived. She was shown walking with a large handbag which was black, hanging from the arm which she held in front of her. She had a noticeable stoop.

"Doesn't she look as if all her bones are knitting together into a hard solid mass?"

"Don't you like her?" I asked.

"You must be joking."

Sunshine streamed through the window and great yellow squares lay across the carpet and up the wall. I glanced sideways, surreptitiously, so I wouldn't be seen. Eva's chin rested on her knees. She had a long nose with a rounded end.

I couldn't possibly have foreseen any of this when, sitting at home, I'd imagined what it would be like coming to see my father.

One evening Eva took me for a walk. We went down to the Thames, to the tow path. Grey still water; ducks floating by and scooping with their yellow beaks; motor cruisers riding by coloured buoys.

We found a bench and sat down. It was a mild evening. We talked about past boyfriends and girlfriends. At some point a man came and sat on the end of the bench nearest Eva. He sat rather too close to her. He took a cigarette from a silver case and lit it carefully.

We couldn't go on talking as we had been so I said, "It's nice here."

"This is where we used to come and feed the ducks when I was a child," Eva replied.

With our eyes we followed a small cruiser moving down the middle of the river.

"We had a boat once," Eva said.

Out of the corner of my eye I looked at the man who had forced himself on us. He was forty-five or perhaps fifty. He had a very long, very unattractive face, very wrinkled, and burning blue eyes. He was wearing a safari jacket which was, curiously, made of leather and brick-red in colour. His fingernails were very long. His head was tilting towards us and he made no attempt to hide the fact he was shamelessly eavesdropping.

"We packed it in in the end," continued Eva in a voice which sounded far away.

At the wheel of the boat, it was now level with us, a man stood smoking a pipe.

"It was cheaper to hire one for the odd day when we wanted one, than it was having it full time. Dad worked this out on the basis of how many days we'd used ours over five years. He really did. He's like that about everything. Gets the cheapest household insurance; buys everything at the Cash and Carry; he'd probably put in a payphone at home if we'd let him. It's nothing to do with being mean. It's to do with being really careful."

She laughed affectionately and our eavesdropper stood up. He looked disgusted. As he stamped away her laughter grew louder.

"Wasn't I good?" she said. "I bored him so much he was driven off."

The wake of the boat, which had passed by, now washed at the bank below our feet. The froth which bubbled on the surface was a yellowish colour.

Retracing our steps towards home, we saw the eavesdropper again. He was ahead of us along the tow path with two youths. One of the youths had a pot belly showing through his tee-shirt and a shaven head. The other was thin and had longish, greasy hair.

The youth with the shaven head, hearing us coming, glanced over his shoulder at us and then turned back to the man.

"Got a cigarette chummy?" he demanded. He made as if to sound polite but the underlying threat was unmistakable.

Out of the pocket of the leather safari jacket came the silver cigarette case. The youth took a cigarette for himself and another for his friend.

"Light," he said with a smirk.

I could see now the older man was trembling as he reached into one of his pockets. He drew out a box of matches and pushed at one end. In his terror he had got the box upside-down and all the matches fluttered out.

"That was very careless," said the youth with the shaven head. Around the heavy, ugly boots which he wore, the white matches with their red tips lay scattered on the ground.

Eva and I were now only a few feet away and the eavesdropper looked at us with his big blue eyes as we approached. He was terrified.

"You'd better pick them up," said the youth and tapped the ground with a toe cap.

Do I tell him not to pick them up or what? I was asking myself when I heard Eva beside me saying, "You're going to miss your bus. You'd better run."

Her order broke the hypnotic atmosphere. There was a moment of silence and then the older man started to run, his safari jacket creaking as he went.

The two youths stared at us with incredulity. We passed, treading the matches underfoot. A moment later they were behind us and I knew that now we were safe. They'd missed their chance and the initiative had passed to us. I realised Eva had her arm through mine and was holding it tightly. In the distance we saw the man in the safari jacket turning through a gate and disappearing.

After we had walked for some while, and felt it was safe to do so, we stopped and looked back. The youths were gone.

"That was very brave," I said.

She shook her head. "Old trick," she said.

"Do you know what our boat was called?" she continued.

"No."

"The Tereva. Teresa and Eva, get it? Tereva. It was Dad's invention, of course. Thank God we got rid of it. It was so embarrassing having that horrible name on the side of a boat."

We laughed and I chased her along the tow path with an armful of cut grass I had found.

Later we went home and studied the timetables of ferry

crossings to Ireland. Eva, Malachy and myself are all going together much later in the summer. We are going to stay in a holiday home which John and Teresa have in county Donegal.

When I was fifteen or sixteen, my English teacher, Mrs Longley, set the class an essay with the title, "Something about Myself". I liked English. I liked writing things for Mrs Longley. Usually I never had any difficulty about just sitting down and doing it. But this was different. I went to my desk at home and found my mind was completely empty. I had absolutely nothing, I realised, to say about myself. I wondered if I could get away with an essay on this theme but I rejected the idea.

All right, I said to myself, let's think about the facts which you do know for certain. Height, weight, age and so on. I made a list which I then tried to write up into something interesting. I tried very hard but it read just like a list. So I tore it up and threw it away.

OK, I said to myself, What's your earliest memory? That's something about yourself. I wrote it down. I was aged, I don't know, two-and-a-half. There was a battered suitcase on top of the wooden wardrobe in my parents' bedroom, the one, I later discovered, where my mother kept her courting letters. This suitcase was covered with coloured stickers. To me, standing on the ground where I was, it seemed intriguing. I wanted it.

The wardrobe door was open. I started pulling on the clothes inside. My intention, I imagine, was to pull myself up. What happened was that the wardrobe toppled, the door frame luckily falling on either side of me, and I found myself suddenly in complete darkness, surrounded by a jumble of shoes, coat hangers, and my mother's dresses which smelt of her scent.

My mother rushed into the room. She wasn't strong enough to move the wardrobe by herself, so she called the fire brigade. They got me out and I was given a severe talking to, surrounded by several grinning firemen in funny hats and waterproof coats. The wardrobe went up and the suitcase went back, only now it went right to the back where it couldn't be seen. There it remained until some years later, when my sisters and I rediscovered it. By this time we were well able to climb onto a chair to reach a potential treasure chest, without killing ourselves.

After I had finished writing this down, I scribbled Mrs Longley's title across the top and sat back. Something about myself? I wondered. This didn't tell anything. It was just an amusing story about the sort of trouble every infant gets into.

I threw it away and started again. I decided, very self-consciously, to do exactly what I thought Mrs Longley wanted. "My parents are fairly good people and they have tried to pass their values on to me," I began (or something like this). "Honesty, thoughtfulness for others, and straightforwardness, are probably what they lay most stress on in the home. I don't know how good I am when it comes to these things, probably not very good, but I make a reasonable effort, I guess," and it continued like this for three or four more pages.

The next English class came round. Mrs Longley entered the classroom carrying our essays. I could feel butterflies in my stomach.

"I've read your work," (it was always "your work" and never "your essays") Mrs Longley began, "and I'm sorry to have to say, I'm intensely [one of her favourite words] disappointed."

Her eyes flicked around the room, her gaze boring into each of us.

"What you have written, class, is what I have been trying to encourage you not to write – clichés – and not just any old clichés but big fat ones about big fat things. Examples of the kind of rubbish I'm talking about include, 'I always tell the truth' (oh yes?), 'I believe honesty is one of the world's most important virtues', 'It is very important to be kind to old people and always to help them across the road'."

Nervous laughter sounded.

"However, the picture was not one of total gloom. There was one outstanding essay. It was Nicola Fricker's."

We were all amazed. It wasn't possible. This spotty, lanky, stupid girl had been singled out for praise by the hypercritical Mrs Longley.

"It is precise, where all the other essays are generalised. It is truthful, where all the other essays are not, despite each carrying at least a paragraph on 'Truth'. But most important of all, it is moving where the others are not. It changed me in some small way, and as I have been trying to communicate, apparently without much success, that is what you are trying to do with your writing. To make something happen to the reader."

She cleared her throat and started to read. The story went something like this.

Nicola Fricker's father was a road construction worker. Every Friday night, after he got paid, he would go to a bar for a couple of hours. When Nicola was thirteen or fourteen, her mother started sending her to this bar to get her father home before he spent too much of his wage packet. Nicola hated the place, smelling of alcohol, filled with smoke. Because of the age she was, her body was changing and there was an unpleasant atmosphere of innuendo.

As the months went by, these Friday-night winkling out sessions developed a pattern. Nicola would arrive. She would find her father. He would never agree to leave immediately. "Have a Coke," he would say, "or a drink if you like," and his cronies would laugh.

Nicola would always say, "No." she would go and sit in the telephone booth and wait for her father. It had a door which she could close. It was quiet. She could sit on the stool alone and she didn't have to put up with any smutty remarks.

Above the handset was a mirror. Looking at it from where she sat, all she could see were the legs of the men standing along the bar or walking by. Judging by their clothes and their shoes and the way they moved, she whiled away her time trying to ascertain the character of these men based on the little she could see.

One evening, in the mirror, she saw a man falling over. He was old and drunk. He lay on the floor, face down, with customers passing but no-one coming to his help. After a while a figure came into view wearing muddy boots and ragged corduroy trousers. The figure pulled the drunk up and got him sitting on his backside.

The drunk's nose was bleeding. The figure handed him down a

handkerchief and then a glass of water. The drunk wiped his face, started smiling and then laughing. He got to his feet and followed the corduroy trousers to the bar.

Nicola wondered who it was? She shot out of the booth and looked at the line of men standing along the bar.

"Hello honey," a familiar voice called out. "Do you want a Coke?"

Standing with the drunk, waving a glass of beer, it was the person she least expected to see.

"No Dad," she said and stood still, neither going forward nor back into the booth.

There was silence. We had all been spellbound, just as if Mrs Longley had been reading from the work of a published author we all admired.

Writing now, in Hampton Wick, I see how clearly a story remains in the mind when everything else goes. I can hardly remember my essay but I'll be telling Nicola Fricker's story to my grandchildren.

Oszkár and his Bride

Teresa's detailed knowledge of the history of her family started towards the end of the First World War. Her maternal grandfather – whose name was Oszkár – was a meteorologist in the Austro-Hungarian army. He was a sergeant. His unit was stationed in what later was to become Yugoslavia.

After four years of war, there were shortages of food. Shortages of everything. To the south, a French–Serbian force was preparing to go on the offensive. The Imperial army was debilitated and exhausted. The enemy would surely reach Budapest. Oszkár and his entire unit deserted.

He walked north. Away from trouble. There was an armistice and in Budapest a government was established under Count Michael Károlyi.

He reached the great plain of Hungry. Rows of Lombardy poplars were planted by the roadsides. The flat fields of sandy earth were bare. The crops of wheat and maize were long harvested. Day after day he walked, unless he could get a lift in a cart pulled by an oxen and driven by a peasant. As he drew closer to his destination which was Budapest, the rumours of chaos, confusion and shortages grew more persistent. So did his sense that all around the country's rim enemies loomed; Slovaks, Rumanians and Yugoslavs – and where else would they go, if they swept in, but of course the capital?

One day, when it was wet and he was sitting against a tree and sheltering under a piece of sacking, he decided on a change of plan. Instead of going leftwards and northwards, he would go rightwards and eastwards, away from civilisation and into what he imagined would be a protective wilderness.

He started and after some days crossed the river Tisza. A fisherman presented him with a small carp. He made a fire with wood from a dead willow and roasted it on the spot. After a diet principally consisting of sour tasting bread, the white, flaky meat was like food eaten for the very first time. Unknown to him then, – he worked this out later – this was the day Hungary was declared a republic. It was November 16th, 1919.

He went on, towards the desolate land known as the Hortobágy. The soil grew whiter, more alkaline, and the water in the wells began to taste more and more as if it had disinfectant in it. For mile after mile there was nothing on the horizon except the crossbeams from which the well buckets hung and long wooden drinking troughs surrounded by trodden earth. Overhead the sky was always a deep grey, reminding him of the colour of gun metal. With each hour he felt as if the sheet of cloud lowered a little towards him. Sometimes he wondered if eventually it would reach him and crush him but he would not let himself pursue the thought.

He began to grow despondent. His original thinking had been to take refuge in the Hortobágy, because it was unlikely he would meet any dangerous humans in such a famously inhospitable area, and also because invading armies would most likely give it a wide berth. Now he began to think about turning back towards, for all he knew, an advancing army, and he hadn't even entered the Hortobágy proper yet.

Sleeping in a ditch one night, he dreamt of a school experiment. Bluebottles in a bell jar. Oxygen was withdrawn. They buzzed and died. Oszkár woke up and decided he wasn't going a step further. He retraced his steps to an isolated homestead he had passed several hours before. When the dawn came, he went in. The owner was a peasant with ten acres. Oszkár negotiated shelter and a daily meal. In return he was to clean the stalls, help with the animals and mend the fence around the farmyard. If he was very industrious he would be taught how to milk the cows. He was to sleep in the barn on the hay.

The following spring, Károlyi's government collapsed. The regime which followed was Bolshevik. The leader was Béla Kún. Oszkár burnt his uniform, dirtied his nails and started to chew tobacco like a peasant. It was not only safer not to go but now he had a reason to stay. The farmer had a daughter and she was pretty. She wore the peasant costume of a bodice and short, bell-shaped skirt reaching only to the knees, which swung as she walked. She took to visiting Oszkár in the barn in the early evenings. While units of Reds galloped northwards towards Czechoslovakia, where they were fighting to regain land occupied by the greedy Slovaks after the Great War, Oszkár and the girl held hands and talked shyly about the future.

Summer came. Every day there was a hot blue sky. It was a time of green and blue dragonflies, darting or hovering, and flies buzzing everywhere in the shimmering heat. This was how Oszkár remembered it when, much later, he told Teresa about it. As it got drier, the earth went whiter but, perversely, here and there were to be found patches of bog. In the alkaline land, these stretches were a virulent, unhealthy green. In the irrigation ditches and the wooden troughs around the well heads, millions upon millions of frogs rapidly bred. They were huge, with swollen bellies and speckled bodies. Oszkár never forgot watching his animals putting their muzzles into the thick, scummy waters of the trough which was alive with them, and from his description Teresa developed a lifelong aversion to frogs.

Inevitably, the Reds came. It was to requisition food. They got the cattle but not the pigs. These were hidden in the barn under mounds of loose straw. Oszkár had taken the additional precaution of binding their muzzles and their feet with twine. A fortnight later the Reds returned. They came quietly and were not expected. This time they got the pigs. They had three women with them: a school teacher of about forty and two girls. They were stripped and raped in the barn and later driven out into the countryside. Oszkár remained throughout their ordeal in the yard, saying and doing nothing. The next time the peasant's daughter visited him, she lay back in the straw and lifted her legs. Afterwards it took an hour with a horse-comb to get all the yellow lengths out of her hair.

The regime of Béla Kún collapsed in August. Whites galloped through the countryside rounding up Reds. Oszkár heard reports of stretches of road where every Lombardy poplar had a dead man tied to it.

One morning, the retributions came to him. He found a man tied upside-down to the crossbar of a distant well. His head had been cut off and bobbed in the water below amongst the frogs and the green scum. There was a placard: *Cut me down. This space needed for another Red.* Oszkár wondered if this was a warning? If he and his boss were suspected of having fraternised? He started carrying a knife and sleeping with a scythe beside him in the hay. But no Whites came looking for him.

He caught the head in a net and brought it out. The peasant thought he recognised the face. It was a Jewish money lender from a nearby town who could never under any circumstances have been a Communist. Oszkár put it in the ground next to the body.

One autumn day, when there was a fine mist drifting across the fields, Oszkár and the peasant went for a walk. When they returned, it was agreed. Oszkár may have been landless but he had an education. His promises had swayed the girl's father. Oszkár and the girl could marry.

The ceremony was a month later. Afterwards, the couple and the guests returned to the farmstead. The bride's mother, who had been silent in church, went to her room beside the kitchen, got into bed and started to sob. Her lamentations could be heard through the wooden wall. When the fiddle players and the accordionist started playing music, everyone forgot. Only the bride remembered. She wanted her mother. She went outside later to get a breath of cold air and shed bitter tears behind the barn. When she told her granddaughter Teresa, years later, about this day, this was her principal memory. Standing in her wedding dress, the perspiration on her face and down her back, chilling in the wind. The sound of the acacia trees stirring, mingled with the music coming from the house. The salty taste of her tears on her tongue.

Oszkár found work as a chemistry teacher in the high school in Mezőtúr, not far from the Hungarian-Rumanian border. It was an overgrown village really, and had not a single dwelling with piped water.

They found a house. It was in a street on the edge of town, with the flat plain beyond. It was like the kind of house to be found in the towns and villages all over the plain. It had stone foundations and was built of bricks of sun-dried mud, which were covered with coarse stucco. This was colour washed a pale green. The house was one storey. There was a cross on the gable end facing the street, and a veranda with doors and windows off it, running along one long wall. The other long wall was blank. Below the veranda lay the garden. It was a private place, over-looked by no-one, except whoever passed by the garden gate.

Outside, in front of the house, there was an earth road, which the wheels of the carts and the hooves of the oxen had turned to mud at the time they arrived. This was January, the middle of winter. On either side of the road there were wide grass verges where geese, with mud spattered on their feathers, searched for food with their yellow beaks and cackled.

They went inside. She lit the stove. One of the seams of the chimney stack had come apart and it smoked slightly. Besides the kitchen, there was a bedroom with a double-bed and a picture of Saint Margaret hanging on the wall, and another smaller room with some tools in it and nothing else. They went and lay down together on the unmade bed. They made love again that night under the picture of the saint. Very soon she was pregnant.

Every morning, before dawn, up and down the street, the peasants who were their neighbours would start the long walk or ride by cart, to the distant plots of land which they farmed. This was the pattern in Hungary, and the homestead where she had grown up in the middle of the countryside was relatively rare. She always woke first and she would lie in bed beside her husband, listening to the peasants calling to one another or their animals, and hearing the wheels of their carts sloshing through the mud. Sometimes she was sick and would have to vomit in the enamel bowl she kept under the bed.

When it got lighter, Oszkár would get up and shave using the piece of broken mirror nailed to the wall by the window, and she would prepare his breakfast: bread and lard, sometimes jam, and bitter ersatz coffee.

After he was gone, she would clean or go to the stores and queue with the only people who seemed to be left behind in the day: old grandmothers who wore black handkerchiefs knotted

tightly over their grey heads and who carried string bags.
Sometimes, as spring approached, the new bride was observed in
her garden, talking to her geese or the hens. When she felt so
torpid nothing was possible, she would go to bed as her mother
had done. But unlike her mother she didn't have to pretend to be
sick. There was no-one at home to have to lie to.

The summer came. The road outside turned from mud to dust.
It rose up in clouds at every footfall, coating one's clothes. In the
garden there were scarlet geraniums, madonna lilies and snap-
dragons. They delighted her. She was only used to sunflowers on
her father's homestead.

On June 5th, the Treaty of Trianon was signed. It settled large
tracts of Hungary on the new Czechoslovakian, Rumanian and
Yugoslavian states. Oszkár was incensed but she felt indifferent.
Six days later she gave birth to a girl. She was the first of the three
children of Oszkár and his wife. And she was the future mother
of Teresa.

Diary, Hampton Wick

I met Mrs Gara, as she is called, on my third Sunday . . .

I stood with the O'Neill family outside a front door. We were on the third floor of a block of flats in Southfields. Teresa pressed the bell.

"Who is it?" said a voice beyond the wood.

"Us," called back Eva. "Me, Malachy, Mum, Dad and a friend."

Behind the pane of frosted glass in the middle of the door hung a piece of lace and behind that I could just about make out the movements of a figure.

There was a long pause as inside chains were unhooked, dead-locks turned and bolts drawn. The door opened back. On the threshold stood Mrs Gara. She had short curly hair dyed brown, small brown eyes set close together, and fat bare forearms.

"Come in," she said quietly, lowering her eyes. It didn't seem like a shy gesture; more like a signal of contempt.

We filed into the living room. It was large with windows overlooking a park. A huge fish tank sat in the middle of a set of empty book shelves. Mercury-coloured bubbles streamed from the bottom.

"Sit down."

Mrs Gara listlessly indicated the leather sofa along the wall and the matching armchairs under the window.

"I was just watching the television. I don't know why I watch it."

The set showed a picture of a man on a bowling green. She pressed the remote control and the picture collapsed into a silver dot.

"This is Malachy," said John. He pointed at me.

"Yes," Mrs Gara said quietly, "you mentioned him on the 'phone. Very nice to meet you." Like her daughter, she spoke English with a strong accent.

"Sit down. Don't make me repeat myself."

Eva was by the fish tank peering through the glass. Inside little yellow and red shapes were darting amongst the greenery.

"The fish are in fine form today," said Eva.

"Better than me," replied Mrs Gara and laughed, the phlegm moving in her chest. She dropped on to the end of the sofa.

I took the straight-backed chair from the wall behind the television. John took one of the armchairs. Teresa sat beside her mother. Malachy sat crosslegged on the floor.

"Can I give them some food?" called Eva.

"Go ahead. Get them fat."

Eva said, "I won't give them much."

Mrs Gara sighed and shrugged her shoulders.

I watched Eva as she tapped the box, and the little particles trickled out and then floated down through the water. I expected a frenzy of activity around the food but the fish seemed supremely indifferent.

"My Harlequin bass died last week," Mrs Gara said.

"What was it?" asked Teresa.

"It was a fish," her mother said.

"What kind of a fish was what I was asking?"

"A Harlequin bass."

John's expression I noticed was a mixture of expectation and dread. Teresa said nothing however, only smiled to herself and shook her head.

"Anyone for a cup of tea?" Mrs Gara asked, lighting a cigarette.

"I thought you'd stopped smoking."

"John?" Mrs Gara ignored her daughter's question and proffered the packet to her son-in-law. He took one.

"Anyone for a cup of tea?" Mrs Gara said again, exhaling.

"I thought you'd stopped," Teresa said again.

"I stopped but then I started again," Mrs Gara told her daughter. "I had a smoking problem because I wasn't smoking. Now I am smoking again, I no longer have a problem."

She crossed her legs and leant back into the sofa. She was wearing pink fluffy slippers with white pom-poms. Mrs Gara, I thought, must be in her late seventies but she looked fifteen years younger.

"Don't make me say it again. Anyone for tea?"

"I'll make it," Eva said. She walked across the room towards the door. She was wearing a black dress. Her shoes were covered with black suede and had tapering heels. They were too large. Her feet slipped about in them making her unsteady.

I listened to the sound of the kettle being filled in the kitchen and the rattle of cups and saucers.

"How have you been keeping?" It was the first time John had spoken.

Mrs Gara jutted out her chin and followed with a hardly audible, half-sighed, "Well. I'm not getting any worse but I'm not getting any better."

"Are you taking the tablets?" asked Teresa.

"Oh yes, I'm taking the tablets. You go into my bathroom if you don't believe me. Great big red ones and blue ones and white ones. Next week they're starting me on some orange ones. There's all the colours of the rainbow on the shelf in there."

"How's the hospital?"

"Don't talk to me about the hospital."

"You go?" said Teresa. John was watching his wife again.

"I never said I didn't go."

"I didn't say you didn't go."

"Teresa didn't say you didn't go," said John, echoing his wife. There was a long pause. Next door Eva was rattling a tin.

"I can't walk very far, as you know," began Mrs Gara, "and I go to the Marsden on Thursday's with Mrs Summers for the radiation treatment, as you also know. We have to be there at 9.30. Last Thursday, as always, she rings the bell at 8.15. I go down. We walk together, very slowly, because I mustn't tire myself. We go by train to Putney and catch the 14. Very nice conductor. He helps us off. He makes sure we're on the pavement before he rings the bell to tell the driver to go. When you have to take public transport and you're sick, you really appreciate a gentleman."

"May I turn on the TV?" Malachy asked. "There's a Fred and Ginger on."

"Sure," Mrs Gara said sweetly.

He took the remote control unit from the table and spun round to face the set.

She continued: "We go into the Marsden. We're on time. We always are. We sit down to wait in the waiting room. The nurse comes over and tells us something about the doctors have been changed. 'Come back at 11.30,' she says. 'But my appointment is for 9.30,' I say. 'What am I to do?' She says, 'The rosters have been changed. I'm sorry. It's circumstances beyond our control. Please come back at 11.30 and you'll have your treatment then.' I say, 'Oh, I see. I'm supposed to go all the way home which will take an hour, and go inside and take off my coat, and then put my coat back on again and come all the way back, another hour, and then have my treatment?' She says, 'I'm sorry.' My God, if I had a pound for every 'I'm sorry' I heard in there I'd be a millionaire. She says, 'If you can't go home, you can wait downstairs. There's a very nice snack bar. You can have a cup of tea.' I say, 'I see, I can just wait around for two hours because you've made a change of plan and haven't the courtesy to tell me in advance. I look old eh? You think because I look old, I can just sit around for two hours at a time and won't mind about it?'"

Mrs Gara spun away the long length of ash she had dropped on to the centrifugal ashtray.

"Don't talk to me about hospitals."

"Don't you think the nurses do a marvellous job?" said Malachy mildly. On the television Ginger Rogers was taking powder from a compact and patting it on her cheek.

Mrs Gara turned in her seat and shouted at the wall.

"How's the tea?"

"Coming," Eva called back.

John said, "What about that leak?"

"Still pouring in. It's coming through the masonry and into the corner above the toilet. I've had to take all the wallpaper off the wall."

"I'll have a look at it later."

"Tea up," Eva said from the doorway.

"That won't do much. It has to be repaired by the landlord."

The castors of the trolley whined as she pushed it across the room. We all watched as she transferred the plates, cups and saucers, the teapot under its tea cosy, and the plate of Cadbury's mini-rolls, to the table. There were also cup cakes topped with glacé cherries and a plate of biscuits.

"Shall I be mother?" said Teresa.

"Yes, you be mother," said Mrs Gara.

Teresa removed the cosy and started to pour. The tea was pale brown. She took off the top and looked into the pot.

"How many bags did you put in, Eva?"

Her daughter at the door said, "Two."

"Is that enough?"

"Let's not worry about it," Mrs Gara said, and added, "Eva, I'll have an instant coffee. Would you do that darling?"

I took a cup of tea from Teresa and stirred it with a spoon.

"How did you come to Britain, Mrs Gara?" I asked.

"How did I come? You mean, how did I travel here?"

"No, Granny," said Malachy, patient but also sounding somehow irritated.

On the set, Fred Astaire in evening dress was climbing a staircase.

"My favourite movie-man," Mrs Gara said, pointing.

"When he says, 'How did you get here?' he's asking by what means you escaped from the clutches of Communism?"

"Didn't they try to stop you leaving?" I asked. "Don't all those Eastern countries forbid their people to leave?"

"Oh no. I'd finished my working life. They didn't want me. I was a burden," said Mrs Gara. "Once you're squeezed dry the Communists don't care."

Eva came back into the room carrying a steaming cup of coffee. Mrs Gara took it and put it down on the low table. The porcelain top was orange. The design consisted of circles with spikes coming out of them.

"Did anyone read about the murder in last week's *Wimbledon Borough News*?"

"I didn't," Eva said, peeling the silver paper off a chocolate roll.

"We don't get that paper," her grandson added.

Mrs Gara produced a newspaper from beside the sofa. I wondered if she'd put it there in readiness? "'Son attempts to murder mother – thirty years,'" she read.

She cleared her throat.

"'Dean Stanton, aged seventeen, was sentenced today at Lambeth Crown Court, to thirty years in prison.   .

"'In June last year, Dean Stanton, a student at Merton College, approached his mother and asked for some spending money.

"'This had been a frequent pattern and Mrs Stanton said "No." In court she described her son's behaviour at the time as moody and irritable.

"'Dean Stanton then began to steal from his mother's handbag. She challenged him on this several times but he always denied it.

"'Mrs Stanton approached the local police. Believing it was the lack of male influence in the house which was to blame for Dean's problems – she was separated from her husband and Dean was her only child – she arranged for a police officer to visit Dean Stanton at the family home. The intention was to talk to the young man, in an informal way, about his responsibilities.

"'Sergeant Nolan, who gave evidence, described how he visited and spent two hours talking with Dean Stanton in the kitchen of the family home. He described Stanton as "receptive".

"'The stealing from Mrs Stanton's handbag, however, continued. Finally, the gas meter was broken open. She announced her intention of reporting her son to the police.

"'Dean Stanton followed her to her bedroom where she went to get a scarf. Dean Stanton pulled her out of the room, threw her through the banisters and down the stairs. He then hit Mrs Stanton repeatedly with a chair.

"'Jon Peters, a friend of Dean's from college, who received a sentence of ten years, was then summoned by telephone to the family home.

"'Peters hit Stanton with the same chair which had been used to hit Mrs Stanton, and then tied him up in the living room. He destroyed objects in the house to create the effect of a violent break-in. Next he telephoned the emergency services. When police arrived, they found Dean Stanton, bloody and beaten, lying tied on the lounge floor. He told police he and his mother had returned and discovered intruders breaking into their gas meter.

"'A perfect crime, only Mrs Stanton was not dead. For four days she fought a life and death battle and finally returned to life from beyond the grave.

"'Dean Stanton was not her natural son but adopted. Speaking after sentence she said, "It has been a nightmare. I'll never adopt again."'"

Mrs Gara folded the newspaper and put it on the low table.

"What about that?" she said. "You bring children up in a loving home. You give them everything. And what happens? They try to kill you."

"It may not have been a loving home," said Teresa quietly. She was staring in the direction of the fish tank at something a long way beyond it. I noticed the three generations of women along the sofa shared the same long noses with round ends and small-boned bodies.

John said, "I think I'll have another cup of tea."

The paper bag under the table rustled and a little black nose appeared at the far end, followed by the body of a white toy poodle. Its fur was so clipped, its reddish skin underneath showed through. It looked about at us, sniffed, and its dainty legs began to tremble.

"Dick, here Dick," Mrs Gara called.

The dog's lip curled and he started to growl.

Malachy left Fred and Ginger driving in a car together, and grabbed the dog from behind. Dick whined, tried to run forward, then turned and snapped at my half-brother with his white teeth.

"Leave him alone," said Eva.

Malachy let the dog go. It scampered forward, growling. My half-brother, on his knees now, growled back.

"Malachy," said Mrs Gara.

He lunged forward, growling and snapping. The dog retreated backwards and then jumped on to the second armchair which was empty.

"Rahah," roared Malachy, raising his arms like an ogre. The animal trembled and lifted his leg. A small stream of yellow pee spattered on to the leather upholstery of the chair. On the television Ginger's ball gown rose as she twirled.

"Look what you've done, you've made him nervous," Mrs Gara shouted at Malachy.

"I'm sorry."

"He never does this. He's completely house trained. Then you come along."

I got up and followed Eva out to see what I could do to help and was followed out by my half-brother.

In the kitchen Eva and Malachy caught one another's glance.

"Naughty," she said, "bad boy."

They started to laugh but held their hands over their mouths and their arms pressed against the sides in order to stifle the noise.

I started to laugh with them.

It was some minutes before we regained our self-composure. Eva filled a bucket with hot water and poured in disinfectant which clouded the water.

I followed my half-siblings back into the living room and just caught the end of what Mrs Gara was saying.

". . . You don't know how to care. You never have. I found out how much you did in the hospital in Budapest."

She tipped a length of ash away and folded her arms like a full-stop at the end of a sentence.

Teresa, to whom she was speaking, was staring into the distance at the spot beyond the fish tank. Her eyes were wet. She lifted her hand and pinched on either side of the bridge of her nose.

"I don't think that's . . ." John started in the equivocal tone of voice which those who've been arguing sometimes adopt when other parties appear.

Teresa gave a shrug and shake of her head in his direction. The message was unmistakable. He closed his mouth and fell silent.

Malachy wet a cloth and wrung it dry. He started to wipe the armchair. The room was filled with the smell of the disinfectant.

"Don't you know how to say sorry?" Mrs Gara asked her grandson, speaking to his back.

"I'm sorry."

For the first time that afternoon Mrs Gara looked pleased.

We left half-an-hour later.

On the way home from her mother's Teresa didn't say anything. She sat beside John in the front passenger seat and stared out the window. I sat with Eva and Malachy in the back.

I hadn't understood what had gone on. What did I know? I was a stranger. I simply accepted something had been said, and now it was casting gloom over all of us.

We turned through the O'Neills' driveway. Gravel sounded under the tyres. John stopped at the front door and we all climbed out.

"I'm going to put this away," John called through the window. He drove forward and turned the wheels towards the two large wooden garage doors.

We followed Teresa into the house. She put her handbag on the hall table. Malachy disappeared.

"Eva," said Teresa, "I have such a headache. I'm going to lie down."

Her daughter said, "I'm sorry."

"I feel so cold," said Teresa from the bottom of the stairs, shivering and rubbing her hands. "Heat me up some consommé, would you?"

She began to climb, one tread at a time.

A depression settled on the house. John did not come in from the garage but stayed there. The sound of hammering occasionally drifted through the walls.

Passing across the landing later, on my way downstairs, I glimpsed Teresa lying on her bed, flat on her back. There was a face mask over her eyes. She was like a corpse. An untouched bowl of consommé was on a tray beside her.

In the kitchen, Eva was at the table, her head resting on her arms.

"What's the matter?"

She said nothing.

I touched her shoulder.

"I always have to do everything when my mother gets like this." Her voice was muffled. She was speaking into the table.

She lifted her head. Her hair was stuck to her forehead and the rims of her eyes were red. She had been crying.

"Dad and Malachy don't do anything when Mum's like this. I do everything."

"Why don't you ask them to help. A question's always free."

"Oh God."

She stared at me.

"I don't know what's going on but you can talk to me if you like."

She turned and looked out the window. I went out to Malachy in the garden. He was pointing an air pistol at a tin can hanging from the bough of one of the apple trees. He squeezed the trigger and the pellet hit. The sound was curiously dead in the open air.

"What happened to Mr Gara?" I asked.

He pumped the lever under the barrel, filling the chamber with air.

"He killed himself."

Malachy fired again and the can swung from side to side like a pendulum.

"Mind you, married to her, are you surprised?"

Mrs Mária Gara

Her first memory dated from an afternoon when she was four or five years old. Because she had been to church in the morning, she had on her best bodice and a bell-shaped skirt, like her mother and her grandmother wore.

It was a warm day in summer. There was a clear blue sky overhead. It was bluest directly above, becoming fainter towards the horizon.

Her father cut some flowers in the garden, and then she walked with him along the street past cackling geese. House after house was still in the midday heat, with slatted blinds behind the windows.

They crossed at the corner. The dust of the road rose in clouds. He fetched her a mug of water from a drink shop which mysteriously was open.

They walked on for some time until they came to the War Memorial. It commemorated those who had died between 1914 and 1918. It showed an angel with an expressionless face cradling the body of a dying soldier whose eyelids were drooping. She had been brought here many times but never before had there been so many people.

Her father gave her the pansies and the marigolds, and she laid them with the other flowers on the steps. Then she followed her father into the crowd. A priest spoke. Prayers were said. A Hungarian national flag was unrolled and hung limply from its pole. Everyone started singing the national anthem but she did not join in. She looked around, first at the feet and the calves of the people, and then upwards. All the men, like her father, wore cheap, dark suits, which hung from their bodies and made them look thinner even than they were, and white shirts buttoned to the neck. One or two had straw hats which they were holding. There were a few women in peasant dress like hers but most wore Western clothes: summer dresses, thick stockings and shoes gleaming with polish. It was a solemn occasion.

After the ceremony ended, her father took her to the main square and bought her a red, syrupy drink from a stall opposite the church. She sat on a bench to drink it and then they went home.

They opened the door from the veranda into the kitchen, and there it was on the wall in front of them. It was the portrait of Saint Margaret from the bedroom. Mária knew the story well. Promised to God by her father Béla, in return for deliverance from the Tartars, she had lived out her life in a convent on an island in the Danube between Buda and Pest, which was eventually named after her.

Beside it hung a portrait of Admiral Miklós Horthy, the Regent. Mária had heard it said of him many times, although she wasn't yet certain she knew what it meant, that he was an admiral without a navy, ruling a kingdom without a king.

Sometimes at night after he had a drink, or now because the service at the memorial had filled him with a mixture of sentimentality and patriotism, her father would salute the portrait.

As Oszkár held his fingers against his temple, Mária saw his eyes were filled with tears. She felt vaguely embarrassed. She slunk behind him. Sometimes, when he got like this, he would lift her up to the portrait and she hated this.

Oszkár was a patriot – or he had become one, on rising to become the principal chemistry teacher in the school. He believed that Horthy was working to regain those lands robbed by the Little Entente – the contemptible union of Yugoslavs, Rumanians and Czechoslovaks – and one day would succeed in getting them back.

Mária, five years old, thought nothing of the Admiral's portrait. In fact she thought he was ugly. Sometimes, when her father was not about, she would stick her tongue out at it. This afternoon, feeling especially daring, she made a face behind her father's back, and ran out into the garden laughing.

Mária was not a likeable child and it was easy to say why. She was quiet and strangely ungiving. This often seemed like churlishness. She had few friends. She appeared to be placid, almost to the point of abnormality, but she was also capable of terrible furies.

At the age of eleven or twelve, she found the rooster pecking at the cake of bread she had left to cool on the veranda. He had stood on it, in order to make a hole in the middle, and his mire lay in little white rounds all over the crust. It was careless to have left it where she had but Mária didn't think about this.

She ran inside, fetched the rake, and ran outside again. She chased the rooster around the garden under the lines of drying paprika, cornering him finally under the walnut tree.

Her mother, hearing screams and frantic clucking, came out to see. She saw the bird scrambling and sending up clouds of dust, swirling feathers, the red coxcomb shaking, the fork rising and falling.

In the evening, Oszkár laid his daughter over the kitchen table and beat her bare legs with a leather strop. Mária's two younger brothers hid under the bed in their room, terrified by their sister's screams.

The next time Mária's feelings overwhelmed her, she was at school. It was in the dressmaking class. A girl she particularly disliked sat on a blouse she was sewing and tore it. Mária picked up a huge pair of scissors and cut off one of the girl's pigtails.

She was sent home. When he returned in the evening and heard the story from his wife, Oszkár decided he would beat her. But when he brought her to the table and saw the little lumps that were her growing breasts showing through her shirt, he knew he would not be able to. He made her write a letter of apology instead.

Mária did not like her mother and especially the way she always seemed to be tired. When she came back from school in the afternoons, she would often find her mother in the chair by the stove. Or sometimes in bed. Her eyes closed and, in a trembling voice, she would complain to her daughter – or her sons if they were there but it seemed particularly to be Mária's sympathy she sought; she would complain about her bones, her aches, her pains, how hard she worked, everything. Mária hated the atmosphere in the house when her mother was like this. Especially if the sun was shining. To avoid it, she would walk home from school very slowly, or arrange to go to study at the home of one of the few friends she had.

When Mária started to menstruate, a new tone crept into her mother's complaints. "Now you are like me," her mother would often say, "you know what it is like." Her mother suffered terribly when she bled – although this wasn't the only reason she went to bed – but to Mária a period was nothing. It happened and it was over. She decided, wrongly, that her mother was making it up. This gave her another reason to reject the older woman, and her dislike began to grow into something stronger.

In relation to her father, the process was in the opposite direction. They grew closer. She excelled at her studies. Particularly chemistry and biology. He helped her. She studied hard. When she was just eighteen, she was awarded a place, along with a small scholarship, at the Eötvös Lóránd university in Budapest. Curiously, she opted to study not a scientific subject but English.

It was 1938 when she went to the capital. It was her first visit. She lived with relatives of her father in a distant suburb of the city and took the tram in each day.

The start of her studies coincided with a time when it seemed all Horthy had been striving for was coming to pass. On September 29th the Munich agreement had been signed. Germany had got Sudetenland, and Hungary certain Magyar-speaking parts of Czechoslovakia. In November, the first Vienna award returned further Magyar-speaking lands, this time from the eastern part of Czechoslovakia known as Ruthenia. In March the following year, whilst German forces moved against the Czech provinces of Bohemia and Moravia, Hungarian troops entered Ruthenia. The newspapers were jubilant. The revision of the Treaty of Trianon was at long last underway. Oszkár's letters expressed jubilation. But not so a young printer whom Mária had met, and whom she was seeing as often as she could. "You wait and see," her young man said to her, "once we get on to this train, we won't be able to get off it."

Three weeks after the German invasion of Poland she discovered she was pregnant. She left her course and became Mrs Gara. The baby was born in the spring of 1940. It was a girl. She was named after her father's mother, Teréza, and later, after settling in England, this became Teresa.

Diary, Hampton Wick

After having a few turns with the air pistol myself, I went back to the kitchen. I found Eva gone. I wanted to suggest we went out, for a walk by the river, or a drink. I went upstairs. Her bedroom door was closed. Teresa called out for a glass of water. I gave her one and went to my room. In the garden Malachy went on firing for a few minutes more and then came in. I heard him later going into his bedroom.

I lay on my bed staring at the ceiling. The lampshade swung gently in the breeze coming through the window.

It got later and the light outside began to fade. It was a slow and creeping process, not sudden. For an hour or so it seemed as if night might never come.

I sat down at the table in front of the window and started to write. Putting down one word after the other, describing the afternoon, I forgot the still sense of gloom in the house.

John went on working in the garage. Very occasionally I would hear the faint noise of banging or a power tool whining. At ten o'clock I heard the back door closing – the wood had swollen in the wet and it made quite a bang when it shut. He called out, "Anyone about?" I listened to him walking around, turning off all the lights. He came up the stairs and I heard his bedroom door opening and shutting. It was quiet again for a while and then came the sound of raised voices. The door on to the landing of the master bedroom opened. Someone came out. Furious remarks were hissed.

I wanted to creep down and look down over the banisters. I told myself "No", but I got up and went as far as my half-opened bedroom door. Then I remembered what my mother always said.

"Never put your nose where it doesn't belong." Not original but effective. I closed my door and went back to the table. I could still hear a vague noise.

The next day I woke up early. The house was still. Then I heard the creak of a floorboard below.

In the small bathroom which I shared with Malachy, I plugged in my shaver. Running the metal nose around my face, I wondered why the little blades inside never nipped the skin? The image formed in my mind of a face with hundreds of little cuts then thousands, made by the merest touch of the whirring blades.

I winced at what I had imagined and took the snout off my skin. I told myself, You're tired. That's the only time you have thoughts like this. I whistled loudly, not allowing myself to think of anything as I finished the job, and went downstairs.

John was in the kitchen at the table. The *Daily Mail* was propped against a jar of marmalade in front of him. He was eating a bowl of Shreddies.

"How are you?"

"I'm well," I said.

On the way down I had seen the door of the little guest room was open. The blankets and the top sheet of the bed inside were tangled. The big alarm clock John used was on the bureau. He had spent the night there. When I came into the kitchen, he must have known I knew. Had the situation been reversed I might have been nervous but he didn't seem to care.

"Sit yourself down." He pointed at a seat and folded the newspaper away.

The clock said a quarter to six.

"You're up early," he said.

"I didn't pull the curtains," I explained, "and the light coming through woke me up."

"We've got to sleep with the drapes like this, . . ."

He held his forefingers side by side.

". . . Teresa and I. One chink of light and it puts her right off."

John got up from the kitchen chair and went to the toaster. He put on two slices of bread and returned.

"Mrs Gara is quite a fierce lady," I said.

"A fierce old gorgon all right," he replied and chuckled.

"Does she always act like she did?"

"She's been like that since the first moment I met her. But her bark is worse than her bite."

"God shouldn't have made her a woman," he continued. "He should have made her a dragon and maybe she'd have met Saint George. She could have gone down fighting and that would have been the end of it."

A spring whirred and the toast came out of the slit. John fetched it back to the table.

"What were you making last night?" I asked.

His face lit up. "Come on."

Holding our pieces of buttered toast we went round to the garage at the side of the house. His workshop was at the back. There was a bench, tools, and tins filled with screws. Wood was piled on a chest of drawers in the corner. Rolls of netting, a pogo stick and a basket with a broken handle hung from the ceiling.

He turned on the working light in its wire basket and said, "There." Beside a washstand stood an old-fashioned single horse plough, with flakes of rust lying around it on the floor and two new wooden handles standing against the wall.

We went back to the kitchen. He poured out two mugs of tea.

"The mother-in-law's a funny old stick you know," he said, stirring his spoon to dissolve the sugar he'd put in.

These weren't quite the words I'd have chosen. Among others, I'd have preferred "malignant" and "venomous".

"Very intelligent, you know," continued John, and his spoon went back on the side of his saucer. "Very educated. University in Hungary. Reads books. Classical music. She hasn't the English though to get it across. It must be very hard for her."

It was probably true, I conceded inwardly. Transplanted to a new culture and struggling to master a second language, she probably came over as coarser than she actually was. On the other hand, her malignancy didn't appear in any way affected. I'd never seen anyone so adept at turning an ordinary remark into the cause of a row, I thought. I didn't pass this on of course but my father must have guessed at it.

"She doesn't mean any harm," he said, "she doesn't know what she's doing."

There was an awkward pause when I tried to think of something to say and couldn't. (All that came to mind, irritatingly, was a long-forgotten phrase, I must have picked it up in a history class or perhaps from my English teacher – "There is nothing intelligent which can be said about an atrocity.")

"I never eat any breakfast," said John finally, "it's a habit from my labouring days."

My father patted his stomach and looked at the clock on the wall.

"I'd have been on the site by now."

"You'll have to tell me about it."

"There isn't that much to tell."

He gave a little half-smile. It was just like him to open up a line of conversation and then, almost as soon as he had done so, to close it down again. I was just beginning to grasp how shy he was.

"Six o'clock," he said. "I'd better be on my way if I'm going to miss the traffic."

He got up.

"The early bird always catches the worm, my mother used to say."

Not for the first time I noticed we were both incorrigible quoters of our mothers.

He put a hand on my shoulder and brought his face down to mine.

"Will you make yourself useful around the place today, if you know what I mean?"

I felt a pleasant warm glow inside suddenly. I was no longer a guest. I was being asked to shoulder my first responsibility as a member of the family. He was counting on me to look after Teresa.

"Yes," I said, I am sure with delight showing on my face.

It was early. Whatever I was going to have to do for the first time as a family member, it was not going to happen for a while.

I got the spare key from its place by the hall mirror and let myself out.

The sky was overcast with grey cloud. There was a breeze. The day seemed wintry.

I walked down Dyson avenue, past the villas and the bungalows, the power boat and a plum tree which grew at the corner. On its branches, some of which had spread over the pavement, hung little hard fruits the colour of greengages. They were months from maturing.

I rambled on to where the railway crossed the main road.

A train passed. I stood under the brick bridge where it was dark and dank and smelt of mould, listening to the clattering of the wheels above, and then to the sighing of the rails as the train disappeared down the track.

A little further on was the station. I strolled past the ticket office and went up to the "down" platform, from where trains went south across the river. Most of the commuters, naturally, were on the "up" side which serves Waterloo.

I found a seat and stared across at them all. The men were mostly in suits; double-breasted jackets, and baggy trousers with turn-ups seemed to be favourites. Hair was uniformly short and looked newly washed. Shoes were usually black and appeared just polished. The women also wore mostly suits; straight skirts and square jackets, and often blouses with bows around the neck. Jewellery glinted; lipstick shone; hair-dos glistened and not a wisp was out of place. Yet every face seemed drawn. Everyone was tired, I imagined, and also irritated because they had had to rush since the moment they had woken.

I felt relief I wasn't one of them, as I made my way down the stairs and into an annex which led to the street.

"Hey."

An oldish man with spectacles and a resentful expression was rapping on the glass of the ticket office. He was inside.

"Where's your ticket?" he called.

"I've only been sitting on the platform."

"Platform ticket then?"

"I don't have one."

He wanted me to buy one. I told him I didn't have any money.

"Go away," he said sourly.

I got back to the house and let myself in.

"Is that you Malachy?"

"It sure is," I called up to Teresa in a cheerful tone of voice.

"Has Malachy gone out?" she called again from above.

I glanced into the kitchen. Another breakfast had been eaten since John and I left.

"I guess so," I called up. "He must have gone to work."

"Can I have the 'phone?"

I unplugged the one in the hall and carried it up. Her bedroom was very dark and smelt of face cream.

"Would you pull the curtains?" she asked faintly.

Mindful of what John had asked me to do, I said, "Sure", but with so much energy I must have sounded shrill.

I found the cord and back the curtains glided.

"Ah," winced Teresa and screwed up her eyes.

The garden lay below; grey earth and lawn.

I pushed in the jack and put the receiver beside her. There was white cold cream all over her face and a head band across her forehead, to keep her hair off it. Overnight she appeared to have aged.

"Tea?"

"Yes," she said quietly.

"How are you feeling?"

She gave a little smile and a shrug.

"I slept well." She didn't sound one bit convincing.

I slipped over to Eva's room and rapped on the wood. There was no answer, so calling, "Eva", I opened the door.

The curtains were open and the room was filled with light. Outside the window the tails of the monkey-puzzle tree dangled down. At first glance there was no sign of Eva, until I looked more closely at the bed clothes.

I prodded through the duvet and found, I think, her ankle.

"Wakey-wakey."

The pillow which covered her head was thrown aside, and she rose upwards like something coming out of the sea.

"God what time is it?" she said rapidly.

"Seven-thirty."

The skin of one cheek was streaked and marked from where she had been lying on her hair.

"I feel grotesque."

She pulled up her knees and rested her chin on them.

"What happened to you last night? I came in from the garden looking for you? I was going to ask you to come out."

"I'd have been terrible company."

"It wouldn't have mattered."

She gave a little shrug.

"Do you ever feel funny about doors and windows?"

I couldn't say I had. I shook my head.

"Sometimes I can't stop myself feeling there's something awful on the other side of them."

"Like in the movies. You open a door – nothing. You fall for ever."

"Not at all. It's something thick and syrupy which I won't ever be able to get out of."

A half-finished skirt and jacket, made from Prince-of-Wales check, hung from the mannequin by the table.

"Nice," I said, airily waving to it.

Eva nodded and I got a small smile out of her.

"I'm going to turn on the kettle," I said, and left.

Walking across the landing I heard Teresa speaking on the telephone in her room.

"This is Mrs O'Neill," she said, obviously speaking into an answering machine. "I'd like to leave a message for Michael Lumley, extension 2851. I have an abscess in one of my teeth today, it blew up last night, and so I shan't be coming into work. It's eight o'clock on the morning of Monday, ... Malachy, what's the date?" she called out to me on the stairs.

Eva went off to work with furrowed brows. I'd agreed to repaint the glasshouse and I spent the morning getting the old paint off with a wire brush. At lunchtime I bought Teresa a cheese sandwich.

"I was dreaming just now," she said. "I was the dresser of a famous opera singer. I gave him his false teeth which he couldn't sing without. But I hadn't noticed they were made of sugar and as he began to sing, they started to dissolve. He was on the stage, the audience in evening dress in the auditorium, his mouth starting to collapse, and I was in the wings, horrified, unable to do anything."

John came home at five. In the evening we ordered pizzas from Pizza the Great. They were brought to the house by a fat blonde woman with very white skin. The tag above her breast pocket gave her name as Cindy.

While John went upstairs for change, this Cindy waited in the kitchen. I offered her a seat but she refused. She stared at the clock and chewed at one of her nails.

"If I don't get my Daniel from the childminder's by eight, I'm in dead trouble," was all she said.

When John appeared, she took the fistful of money he held out without counting it and rushed from the house, leaving behind her hat, order book and handbag.

Teresa took her dinner in her bedroom. That left four of us in the kitchen. We ate off the formica table. It was light outside but the neon strip hummed overhead.

The pizzas had a thick base of dough that was white and spongy. Each one was covered with the thinnest smear of tomato purée which had bled into the crust underneath. The mushrooms were black like old bruises. The slivers of ham were shiny and plastic. The mozzarella was exaggeratedly white and stringy. It stuck doggedly to the teeth like old bubble gum.

"That wasn't bad," said John, pushing his knife and fork together when he'd finished.

He was the only one of us who did manage to eat it all.

I went to bed early.

In the middle of the night I was woken up by voices coming from below, and laughter. My watch said half-past three.

In the kitchen I found Teresa and Eva, sitting at either end of the table. Two red candles burnt in silver candlesticks. There were opened tins of food everywhere. They were drinking champagne. Eva was wrapped in a towel. Teresa wore a pink towelling dressing gown.

"We're having a midnight feast," said Eva.

"Supper was so disgusting," Teresa added. "Come and sit down." She's drunk I thought.

Eva started to pour a glass for me.

"Whoops." Froth rose above the rim and trickled down the sides. She lifted the glass and licked the excess off the stem.

"Waste not, want not."

Eva was drunk too.

I took the glass.

"Cheers," they said.

The champagne prickled the tongue as it ran towards the throat. I spread some tuna fish and cold sweet corn on a piece of Ryvita.

Later Teresa tuned the radio to a station in Holland and made me waltz with her to Steeley Dan singing "Ricci Don't Lose That Number", while Eva called out, "Right foot, left foot, right foot, left foot, right foot . . ."

The birds were singing when I climbed the stairs back to my room. The two women were still in the kitchen. I got into bed. Across the suburbs came the sound of a train rumbling along. The noise was reassuring.

I thought about Teresa and Eva. There was something about these two which left me with a faint sense of dread. It was not an unfamiliar feeling. I'd known it before at school when I rubbed up against those hopeless cases who cheated at exams so ineptly, exposure was inevitable; or drank so stupidly getting into a pointless fight or driving into a tree was inevitable. They were out of control and so in a different way were the mother and daughter.

I didn't like that. I don't like anything to be out of control. I like everything just so.

I strung up the badminton net between two apple trees. I was probably wearing my Princeton university tee-shirt. The grass was wet and pretty soon there was damp around my toes.

Eva was on the other side of the net. She wore a large tee-shirt and a sweat band to keep her hair out of her eyes. She also had on her spectacles. She was short-sighted. They were large with black rims and worn with a cord in case they fell off.

Eva's playing was deceptive. When she was waiting to receive a service or return, she appeared to shake slightly. She gave the impression of being not quite in control physically. When she swung the racket it seemed to waver which reinforced this impression. Yet when she hit the shuttlecock, it was with great force and accuracy. Her own serves went very high. She beat me decisively.

Although I am quite competitive I didn't care. What mattered was being with her. I remember everything about that hour, writing now, with great clarity. The smell of the grass and the earth. The noises of the neighbours as they got up, filtering from the surrounding houses. Eva waiting on the far side of the net, her head tilted slightly to the right.

We finished around nine o'clock. Eva went off to get ready. She had to go to her job in a local drug store, or chemist as I was learning to call it.

I went in and sat down at the kitchen table. The copy of the *Daily Mail* must have arrived and I probably opened it.

Mrs Gamage, who came to clean the house on Saturdays, was standing at the sink. She was washing the huge pan used for grilling. There was that soapy, sudsy smell I always connect with washing-up.

Teresa was in an apron kneeling on the floor. She opened the door of one of the low kitchen cupboards under the worktop and took out several biscuit tins, a pile of old telephone directories, and rolls of picture wire. She was going to wash the shelves and line them with paper.

"Malachy," she said, "would you like to do something for me?"

She was holding a plastic bag.

"Would you please bring this round to the pizza place?"

I looked into the bag myself.

There were the purse and the belongings left by the girl who had brought us the pizzas.

Pizza the Great was on the other side of the bridge in Kingston, and quite a long way down the High Street.

As I came up to it, I saw its doors were shut and it looked dark inside. Of course it would be closed, I realised. It was just after half-past nine.

Drawing closer, I noticed some sort of movement inside. I put my face against the glass. A black girl was mopping the floor. She was in the red flared trousers and the red striped waistcoat which all the employees wore.

I rapped on the glass and shouted, "I've got something for someone who works here."

With a movement of the hand she indicated I was to go around to the back.

Here I found a door. I pushed it open. There was a long corridor with a filthy floor. There were boxes of tomato purée and sacks of oven-ready chips piled at the side. There was the smell too which I remember from my own time working in fast food restaurants as an adolescent. It was of old grease, human sweat, and a washing-up powder which has a special, pungent industrial smell.

I went through to the kitchen. Several employees were standing in a circle. I put my head over someone's shoulder and saw they were all looking at a dead rat lying on the floor.

A small Chinese man frowned and stepped forward.

"Yes," he said.

On his breast he wore a badge which gave his name as Timothy. He had won four credit stars.

"I have some things which I think belong to someone who works here. She made a delivery and left them at the house, a week or two ago."

I got out the order book which had written in big letters on the outside, Cindy.

"She doesn't work here any more," Timothy said. He added somewhat mysteriously, "We had some problems with her."

He didn't think she was likely to call in and he wondered if I wouldn't mind bringing her things around to the flat where she lived. It was only a few minutes walk away, he said. I agreed.

Cindy lived on the Dickens estate. Her block was called Copperfield house. Like all the other blocks, it was built of brick and about five storeys high. There was a balcony in front of each apartment and these were mostly crowded with drying laundry and cardboard boxes.

I climbed the stone stairs to the third floor. The door of Cindy's flat was yellow. I pressed the bell.

"Yeah. Coming," a voice shouted inside.

The door opened and there was Cindy. She wore a nylon housecoat open at the front over a lilac-coloured nightdress. She had shoulder-length hair which had been dyed with peroxide. Her face was made up.

"Did you telephone?" First Timothy's and now this mysterious remark.

"No."

"Oh."

"I've got something for you."

"Oh."

"When you made a delivery some weeks ago, you left these at our house."

A look of recognition was creeping across her face.

"I know what you've got. Come in."

In the small hall there was a big poster on the wall showing three kittens playing with balls of wool. It was entitled "Playtime".

She looked into the plastic bag and said, "Thank you so much."

"You're welcome."

"I'd like to offer you a cup of tea, but I've got no milk."

She asked me where I was from. I told her and we talked for a couple of minutes.

Suddenly she reached out and touched my chest. I thought there must be something on my tee-shirt and she was brushing it away. Then she went on touching me and I realised she was stroking my nipple. I could feel it growing hard.

I had a curious sense that I was seeing myself from above, standing in the dark hall with this plump woman before me, her arm out-stretched and her hand on my chest.

It only lasted a moment and then I returned to myself and took a step back.

"Twenty quid love."

"No," I said and left quickly.

I was all right on the stairs but by the time I reached the street, my legs had begun to tremble.

Teresa

Teresa was one and a half years old when her country went to war. Two days after the Germans sent their armies over the border into the Soviet Union, the Hungarians followed them.

She grew up with blackouts and immense queues for food, and mostly without her father. Stephen had been conscripted but after basic training had begun working as a printer on the army newspaper. When the news of this posting came, Teresa watched her mother dance around their room, although she did not understand what was happening.

Teresa and Mrs Gara lived together in an outlying suburb. A shabby archway led from the street to the courtyard of their block. This was overlooked by the windows of all the flats. Through an entrance with no door and up dark stairs led to a second-storey landing where they were.

It was a single room with one window. There was a cold tap in the corner with a long stone sink underneath, and a stove for which they never had enough fuel to keep going all the time. The lavatory was near the stairs, shared with all the others on the landing. Teresa slept with her mother in the bed, except for those very occasional times when her father came home. Then a screen was put up and she slept on the floor.

Every weekday, from the time Teresa was one, Mrs Gara left her with an old woman who lived on the other side of the courtyard, and travelled to the university. She worked there as a laboratory assistant. Teresa spent her days playing with other children on the staircases, or queueing with the old woman for food or fuel.

Her earliest memory was from the time she was four. Suddenly there were new soldiers in the streets of Budapest, and there was talk of someone called Szálasi. At the time she did not follow what was going on and it was only later she understood: the Germans had occupied the country and appointed a puppet.

In the district there was a branch of the German Red Cross. Clothes were distributed from here. One Sunday she stood with her mother for hours on the icy cobblestones outside, and for their pains they were given an evening gown.

When they got back to their room, Mrs Gara tried it on. She found it was an almost perfect fit.

It was nearly Christmas time. Teresa's mother was invited to a party. Teresa did not understand exactly what this was. Only that it was an event.

On the evening it was to happen, her mother hurried home from work. Teresa watched her wash her small, naked body with a flannel and a pan of warmish water. Every time a splash went on to the floorboards, it turned their colour from light to dark brown.

Clean underwear lay on the bed beside Teresa, and a pair of silk stockings, still in their tissue paper, hoarded from before the war.

After her mother had washed, she soaped her legs and shaved them with a safety razor, scraping and then agitating the silver shape in the water. She did the same to her forearms. Because it was so quiet, Teresa could hear the bristles rasping.

Her mother gave Teresa the bowl to empty. Taking care not to spill any of its contents, she carried it slowly across the landing. She put the bowl down on the ground and turned on the light in the lavatory. She poured the water away. It was grey and soapy and filled with little dark, black flecks.

She went back to their room. Her mother had combed her hair and pinned it up, and was inserting her small gold earrings. Teresa rinsed the bowl in the sink. Her mother, still naked, stood in front of the tiny face mirror which was the only mirror they had, and began to smooth down her eyebrows with her spit. She had a little powder and a little lipstick. When she turned away from the mirror some minutes later, her cheeks were whiter and her lips were redder than Teresa had ever seen them before. Now she painted on her nail varnish and stood for several minutes in the middle of the room, holding her hands at arm's length and waving them about.

Teresa's mother put on her underwear and then put on a pair of gloves to pull on the stockings. At last she got into the evening gown. It was black. It went all the way down to her feet. It was supported by two fine bands which left the arms and most of the shoulders bare. The full skirt swished when she moved.

Her mother pulled on the woollen coat she wore every day. It was shiny and the little holes all over it had been darned with different coloured threads. The new dress showed incongruously below the hem. The old woman with whom Teresa stayed in the day came in. The old woman and her mother talked for a few minutes.

Teresa was asleep when her mother came back. She spoke angrily and the old woman, sitting by the bed, left the room hurriedly. Teresa sat up in bed. By the light of a candle, she watched as her mother unbuttoned her dress at the back, and kicked it under the bed. It was puzzling and alarming. Her mother threw herself down beside Teresa and, with her face pressed into the pillow, started to sob.

Not long after, there were footfalls on the landing and a ferocious banging on the door. Teresa watched her mother pull on her coat and open the door. Men came into the room; some were soldiers, others were not.

The dress was pulled out from under the bed – it was covered with dust, and shown to one of the men. He started shouting. Teresa was frightened. Her mother found her documents in a drawer and showed them to the man.

Teresa and Mrs Gara both dressed and were brought by the men to a police station. The man who had shouted brought the dress with him. They remained in the station all night in a room with a single wooden bench, and plaster walls pitted with holes, and scrawled with names and hopeless messages. In the morning they were allowed to leave but Teresa noticed the evening dress was not returned.

While they waited for the tram, she asked her mother about it. "Never ask," her mother replied and then wiped her daughter's red nose.

Teresa did not find out the whole story until much later, and it was her father who told her.

The party to which her mother had gone was in one of the university's halls. In the chandeliers, candles flickered. Wandering around, Mrs Gara began to notice she was receiving strange looks. Every time she tried to talk to someone she knew, they hurried away. Finally a colleague whispered. 'How could you?' 'How could I what?' she asked. 'Look at your front,' he said.

She ran to the washroom. When she got before the full-length mirror, she saw what was wrong. Most of the clothes the Red Cross had had once belonged to Jews, and she saw now her evening gown was no exception.

Just as a picture which has been on a wall for a long time, always leaves a box-shape of clean paint after it is taken away, so, plainly visible on the left breast – obviously the fabric here had aged less when the symbol had been in place – was the shape of the Star of David.

Whenever she remembered the event in later life, Teresa always had the same reaction. How lucky she and her mother had been in the police station that night, she would think, for as she knew only too well, many, many people in Hungary at that time had been killed for far, far less.

Margaret

She was John O'Neill's mother. She was from Kildare originally. The family lived not far from Athy, farming ten acres and keeping a cow. Their house was a white-washed cottage with two rooms. In the larger room, a turf fire burned continuously. The family's hair and clothes were never without the smell of the smoke.

James Malachy Garrett was the man of the house. He was a plump figure with a moustache who wore a bowler hat on Fair days. Matilda was his wife. She had eyes which were grey and she kept her long black hair hidden under a mob cap.

At the time their difficulties started, there were three children; John-James was ten; Helena was six; Margaret the youngest was two. Their difficulties were the old ones in Ireland. Too meagre an income even to subsist on. In 1898, for the third year in succession, James Garrett defaulted on his annual rent.

One October morning, Margaret sat on the earth floor of the cottage. Beyond the small, glassless window, rain streamed from the ragged edge of the thatch.

The sound of marching feet drifted from the lane beyond the field. Margaret ran to the half-door and looked out. Beyond the alder trees which lined the road bobbed the blue pointed helmets of the police and the dull barrels of their rifles.

John-James, who had been posted to keep a watch out, was running towards the house shouting, "Peelers".

With nowhere to go, James Malachy Garrett's plan was to attempt to withstand a siege. He drove their cow, wide-eyed with terror, past Margaret into the room. The animal immediately loosened its bowels on to the earth floor. John-James followed with the chickens, clucking and screeching. The rooster flew up into the alcove beside the chimney breast and started to crow.

Margaret watched as her father closed the half-doors. As there were no bolts, he had cut staves of alder which he wedged behind them.

Into the window he put a butterbox which he had set aside. It filled the entire space. The room went dark except for the embers glowing in the hearth.

Her father started to nail the butterbox to the window ledge, using the hatchet as a hammer. As the blows sounded, Margaret felt a sensation in her stomach which she had never known before. She wanted to pee but it was out of the question going to the place behind the byre which they used. She would have to hold it.

She ran to her mother who was under the table with the other children and wriggled onto Matilda's lap.

Her mother prayed while in the bedroom her father nailed a second box into the other window.

He came back into the room.

"We're safe," he said and crawled under the table to his family.

Outside the sound of marching feet became distinct, and grew louder as the constabulary approached. Margaret could hear their dog barking and she wondered how they had forgotten to bring him in.

A voice called out an order and the marching stopped. In the silence which followed, there was just the howling and the yapping and the faint sound of the rain falling on the thatch above. Then came a dull thud and a terrible yelp and Margaret couldn't hear their dog any more.

Now Margaret heard voices calling. They were calling for her father. James sat quite still beside his wife and said nothing.

The voices stopped. For a long time nothing seemed to happen. Margaret began to wonder if that was perhaps the end of it. If the men outside had gone away. She wanted her father to open the door and the window and for daylight to stream in.

Margaret lay with her head against her mother's breast. It was the safest, warmest place she knew. She smelt her mother's smell. It was flour and the meaty smell of the cow's udders and the potato skins which Matilda mashed up every day for the chickens with sour milk, all mixed together.

Then Margaret realised the men outside had not gone away but simply dropped the level of their voices to a quiet susurrus. Her eyes began to smart. She coughed. John-James and Helena coughed. Her mother and father coughed. Even the cow coughed and bumped against something in the corner. She sensed the room was filled with smoke.

"They've blocked the chimney," her father suddenly exclaimed.

He crawled out from under the table, found the bucket and threw the water it held on to the fire. There was a great hiss and the red embers turned to black. The room went even darker.

Through the tears in her eyes, Margaret saw the tiny line of silver where the daylight seeped through the crack in the middle of the butterbox. If only she could be outside, she thought, and putting her face against her mother, she gave a long sob.

Margaret heard more shouting and then a terrible banging began. There came the sound of rending wood and the box disintegrated. The pieces flew through the air and landed on the floor with a clatter. Daylight flooded in and there, framed by the window, was the face of a constable. He was holding the axe he had used to smash the butterbox.

A moment later the door crashed open. There was an instant of stillness and then four policemen rushed in carrying rifles with long bayonets attached to the end. Two of them knelt and pointed their guns at the Garretts. The other two chased the cow round the room until she ran through the door into the rain dropping great pats after herself.

A sergeant told them to leave. Outside a fine grey drizzle was falling. Margaret felt a few wet droplets on her face. Matilda covered her with the end of her shawl.

There was a big oak tree at the side of the house and they were made to stand there. Rain dripped from the slime-green branches. A small crowd gathered at the bottom of the lane to watch. One or two shouted abuse at the Crown forces.

The police carried out the contents of the house: the table, the stool, the cooking pot, the settle bed and the two sacks filled with straw which were the mattresses, the washing line from the chimney breast and the clothes on it, the sack of potatoes, the stone jar of milk, the packet of salt, the bar of soap and the two tallow candles, and put them all on the flagstone in front of the house. They tethered the cow and tied up the legs of the chickens, so they could not run away. They erected a tripod twelve feet high and swung a heavy beam from it. They battered at the gable end of the house behind the hearth. With a crash the stones came tumbling down and a cloud of dust rose in the air. A moment later the roof beam hit the ground. There was a terrible crack as it snapped in the middle. Thatch flew everywhere.

Now the house was uninhabitable, the RIC had finished their job. They formed into a column two abreast. Some of them carried chickens under their arms. The sergeant at the rear was holding the rope tied around the neck of the cow. He advised the Garretts they had to leave. Then he marched his men past the crowd and into the landscape on which the drizzle was steadily falling.

In exchange for the settle bed, a neighbour gave the Garretts an old turf cart and an ancient grey donkey with leathery patches of skin all over his thin legs. James stood the table on the cart to form a cover. The family's possessions and the children went underneath in the dry.

It was the middle of the day when they started. By the evening they had reached Cloney, ten miles to the north. There was a small grey public house on the outskirts of the village. James insisted he needed a drink and went in. When he came out, half an hour later, he had spent all their money. In Monasterevin – which they reached the next day – he had to sell his silver fob watch and Matilda's plain gold wedding ring.

The family made their way north and west, through Westmeath, Longford, and Leitrim to Donegal in the far north-western corner of Ireland.

Here, their luck turned. They found twenty acres to rent above Glendowan in the Derryveagh mountains. It was hilly, boggy land which could only support a cow and a few sheep. The farmstead was a low grey-stone building with a roof of grass sods cut from the mountainside and laid on boards covered with tree bark.

The previous occupants had been sheep and the family's first task was to shovel out their compressed droppings and pile them behind the dwelling.

It was James's intention to use the droppings on the land but this never happened. They remained where they were. Other rubbish from the house was thrown on top. The children trampled everything together and a hard pile formed.

When James returned home drunk, which was most Saturday nights, searching for the back door in order to make a discreet re-entry into the house, it would often trip him over. Margaret and the other children and Matilda, all awake while pretending to be asleep, would listen with their hearts beating. If James cursed as he struggled to get to his feet his temper would be awful. When he got into the house he might shout, or hit, or fall into the settle bed with Matilda and do the thing and make the noises which Margaret found so troubling.

On the other hand, if he laughed, or sang as he rolled on the heap, that was good. The worst that would happen then was that he would light the candle, get them up and sing songs and talk for half of the night.

Once, he broke a bottle in the fall and Margaret heard her father weeping. To her and everyone else's relief, instead of coming into the house, he disappeared into the night. He did not return for four days. When he did, he was drunk and barefooted. His wife never asked him where he had been or what had happened to his boots and Margaret never found out.

When she was eighteen years old Margaret walked to Londonderry and bought her first pair of shoes. They were black with silver eyes and long brown thin leather laces.

Outside the shop she put them on immediately and walked proudly towards the quays. Having gone barefoot all her life it was not long before her feet started to ache.

At the office of the Erin Steamship Packet Co., she bought a third-class ticket, one way, to New York. She was lucky. Her boat was one of the last to cross the Atlantic before the outbreak of the First World War.

On arrival, Margaret and the other emigrants on board were disembarked on to Ellis Island for processing. When a doctor indicated that he needed to perform an examination for venereal disease, Margaret fainted. Coming to, two or three minutes later, she found her clothes were in disarray. She was certain the worst had happened. Her first months with her cousins in Brooklyn were a nightmare as she waited for the tell-tale signs of pregnancy. Only after the ninth month had passed did she finally believe she was safe.

When the war ended, Margaret returned to Ireland on holiday. She arrived at the farmstead above Glendowan wearing a large hat with feathers, grey stockings and carrying a muff. She had dollars.

While she had been away, her mother Matilda had grown more stooped and grey. Her father James had grown stouter and more subdued. Helena had married an RIC constable and she lived with his people on their small holding near Welchtown. John-James, her brother, was still living at home. He was twenty-eight and a bachelor. He maintained this suited him well. As a Nationalist and a physical-force man a wife would have been an encumbrance, he said.

Margaret went to a dance in Letterkenny. She met a man called Walter O'Neill who had a lorry. He drove her home in the early hours of the morning stopping at every public house along the way for a drink. Not once did he ask her to join him but left her waiting each time, alone, in the cab.

Four weeks later they married. Friends and relatives of the Garretts applauded Margaret on her catch. Walter was a prosperous farmer from Church Hill. An uncle, a Catholic priest, had settled on him a house and several hundred acres. What Walter got was a beauty, who was not afraid of hard work.

After their honeymoon on the Donegal coast at Bundoran, the couple travelled to New York. Walter worked as a conductor on the elevated railway, feigned great unhappiness at being in a city away from his beloved fields, and drank every night in the Irish bars.

When Margaret lay in bed waiting for the sound of his stumbling footsteps on the stairs she remembered lying on the floor as a child, waiting for the noise of her father returning from the pubs in Glendowan.

At the sound of Walter's key in the door, Margaret's heart would start to race – just as when she was a girl – and she would strain her ears, trying to gauge from the noises he made whether he was likely to be violent or amorous. She was not quite certain which was worse: being struck or their brief joyless couplings.

In the newspapers stories started to appear from Ireland of bombings, murders and outrages. The number of incidents accumulated until it was undeniable – the country was at war. On one side were Crown forces – the British army and the Royal Irish Constabulary in which her brother-in-law served – and on the other the Sinn Feiners with whom her brother sided.

Each day when she came home from Saks department store, where she worked in the haberdashery department, Margaret went to the local parish church in Brooklyn to pray for peace. With her sister's husband on one side and her brother on the other, she could not take sides.

The letter was waiting for her when she got back one boiling Saturday afternoon in July. She recognised her sister's handwriting immediately and her heart started to race. She tore it open and read.

Her brother-in-law had been travelling in a Crossley tender. Among the other passengers was a drunken Black and Tan. He had omitted to put on the safety catch on his rifle. When the lorry went over a bump the gun had gone off and blown Thomas's head off.

Further letters from home were filled with accounts of the family farmstead above Glendowan and how it was turned over incessantly by the Crown's forces. John-James was wanted for the shooting of a magistrate. They never found him in the house because he was on the run, hiding in the Blue Stack mountains with half-a-dozen other men

A year later the truce was signed. Margaret was jubilant. Her brother had survived even if her brother-in-law had not. When she went home to Ireland with Walter, she could be certain John-James would defend her.

In the course of a row, later that summer, she shouted this out. "Ha," Walter had shouted back derisively, and from his pocket he had drawn out a letter. Matilda had directed it to him because she thought it was better he broke the news verbally to Margaret than that she got it cold, from a letter. The envelope and its contents were very crumpled. Walter had been carrying it around for over a fortnight. He read it to his wife.

The day after the signing of the truce, wrote Matilda, John-James had gone to Lough Swilly to try some blast fishing. His Mills bomb had gone off prematurely and blown a hole the size of a football in the middle of his body. Twelve hours later he was dead. As a serving Captain in the Irish Republican Army, he was buried with full military honours.

Walter took the death to heart as if it was his own brother who had died. He was quarrelsome and bad tempered at home but justified his behaviour as the consequence of his grief. He drank heavily and told the story to anyone in a bar who would listen. His narrative was spellbinding. Sometimes he could make strangers weep.

Margaret brooded on her grief alone, telling no-one except the Parish priest.

In Ireland the Treaty was signed and soon the country was at war again. Having won the right to self-government from the Crown, the Nationalist victors now fell out amongst themselves on the terms of the settlement, by which six counties in the north of Ireland had remained British, while the remaining twenty-six had come to them. The fight between the pro- and anti-Treaty forces was a true Civil War. When Margaret became pregnant, Walter agreed to her suggestion that they postpone their return.

In 1922 a son was born. In the bar where Walter found himself that night, he bought drinks for everyone. He did not return home for a week although he reported to work every day.

The anti-Treaty forces were gradually worn down and some sort of normalcy returned to Ireland. Half-way through the decade, Margaret and Walter came home and and settled in the house at Church Hill.

It was an old, three-storey dwelling of grey stone with a grey slate roof. There were mice everywhere and speckled patches of brown in the corners of the bedrooms.

Margaret travelled the country, buying old furniture at auctions and house sales. She bought a bed with a carved rosewood head, a chaise-longue covered with bottle green velvet and an enormous glass-fronted cabinet for the parlour. She filled this with the china and the glassware she had brought back home from New York.

The first-born child, whom they had named Peter, was followed by two further children, Maureen and Kathleen. They were born before the end of the decade.

Margaret, her child-bearing duty done, now took to bringing the girls into bed to sleep with her. Walter moved into the small bedroom behind the kitchen. This was where the hired hand would have gone, had they had one.

The reason they hadn't was they couldn't afford him. Because of a combination of mismanagement and Walter's drinking sprees, which would take him away for weeks, sometimes months, Fort William – as the house and demesne were known – had gone to the dogs.

Most of the land he had either given away or sold to pay off his drinking debts. In the nucleus of fields around the house which was all that was left, ragwort and weeds thrived; many of the fences were fallen; the streams were blocked and muddy.

They lived off the sale of fresh eggs produced by Margaret's chickens. These she sold to a greengrocer in a prosperous part of Londonderry. Walter began to develop a purple nose from his drinking.

Then came the war. The six counties which were British were only twenty miles away. Margaret went on selling her eggs across the border; they took all she had, as well as bread, butter and newly hatched chicks. Walter sold milk, bacon and hay. But what the O'Neills made from the sale of all this produce was nothing in comparison to Walter's profits from selling tyres, car batteries and spark plugs on the black market. He went across the border loaded with these twice, sometimes three times a week. He had a special suitcase with a false bottom and a coat lined with false pockets. He was never caught.

One night, inflated with his new wealth and aroused by a full bottle of Three Barrels brandy, Walter entered the room where Margaret now slept alone.

Neither her age, which was forty-five, nor the piece of sponge, which she stuffed into her dry sex, protected her. She conceived, and in the spring the following year, bore her fourth and final child. She called him John-Michael after her brother. The name was later shortened to John.

Diary, Hampton Wick

I followed John and Malachy into the workshop at the back of the garage. The plough stood in the middle of the floor on pieces of paint-spattered newspaper. The two wooden handles were so new they looked almost white. The metalwork was a dull black and the blades were bare, silvery coloured, except for the cutting edges where they were tipped with red.

John drove the car out on to the gravel in front of the house and we draped a blanket over the roof rack. Together we all lifted the plough – I don't know how much it weighed but it was very heavy – and carried it out, making short mincing steps. Finally, we heaved it on to the roof.

"Have fun," Malachy said to us and, dodging round his mother who was standing in the way of the open front door, disappeared into the house. He wasn't coming.

"Have a good time," Teresa called over without much enthusiasm. John, already in the front seat of the Sierra, pulling the safety belt over his body, acknowledged his wife with a wave of the hand.

"I hope you do enjoy it," Teresa said, this time to us, to Eva and myself, standing in front of her on the gravel.

"Don't forget, I'm relying on you," she continued quietly.

"Mum," Eva called back, while at the same time widening her eyes. "I can't make any promises," she continued quietly so that only her mother could hear. "If you're so worried, you come."

John gave two small toots on the horn and wound down the driver's window.

"Come on," he called.

"You just go and enjoy yourself," said Teresa and gave a nervous smile.

Eva opened the passenger front door and motioned to me to get in.

"Don't you want to ride there?" I asked but she didn't.

She hopped into the back and closed the door.

'Don't do anything I wouldn't do," John called to his wife and we nudged through the gate into the road.

"'Bye," Teresa called from behind, and turning the corner I caught a last glimpse of her through the rear view window, waving with one arm while the other was held across the stomach. Malachy stuck his head around the lintel at that moment and then they were gone.

John drove along Dyson avenue slowly and turned carefully at the corner. It was a still summer's evening and sunlight yellowed the brickwork of the houses we glided past.

"You're really going to enjoy yourself tonight," Eva said to me archly. I turned and saw her run a lipstick around her mouth and then roll her lips. The car interior was filled with its sweet smell. "A real Irish knees-up and probably a punch-up."

"Don't pay any attention to her," said my father from behind the wheel and he laughed quietly.

Our destination was a public house in Wembley called The Plough. The doors were blue and scuffed, especially along the bottoms, and the glass in the windows was opaque.

On the side of the pub a sign read *Patrons' Car Park*. John negotiated the Sierra down a tiny, bumpy alley. I could hear our tyres sluicing through puddles below.

John parked beside a battered van and went off to find someone to help us. He returned with an enormous man who had piercing blue eyes and curly hair. This was Pat.

We got the plough down and carried it into the saloon bar. Pat indicated the piece of cardboard on the floor where it was to go.

Once it was down I could take in our surroundings. The bar in the centre was 'U'-shaped with glasses hanging from racks above. The stucco ceiling was painted pea green. The red velvet seats around the edges of the room were pock-marked with blobs of chewing gum.

A man came up with a flushed face and a bald head.

"This is Malachy, my son," said my father tentatively. I saw a flushed hand that went with the flushed face coming towards me "And this is Dan," my father continued, pointing at the man.

"You're welcome," Dan said, "what'll you have?"

Not knowing what to say, I looked at the shelves behind the bar in case there was a bottle which caught my attention.

"Whiskey and a Guinness?" he suggested.

"OK."

"Brandy and soda," said John.

"White wine," said Eva.

On the floor behind the counter, a young boy, who looked about sixteen years old, was stacking tonic water bottles on a shelf. Addressing the young man as Paul, Dan ordered the drinks.

While we waited for them to come, we all turned and looked at the plough.

"Beautiful," Dan said, "I'm going to put it there."

He pointed to an empty corner of the room. "It'll be a feature."

"Pointa Guinness Paul agus paicead crisps,' said a man at the bar in Irish.

"Cén blaisiu?"

"Salann 's finéagar."

The drinks appeared. We all held up our glasses to toast one another. I saw then something I'd never seen properly before. John drinking. He put the glass to his lips and poured the brandy down in one go. He put the empty glass down on the counter and Dan called out to Paul, "Another brandy and soda. Make it a large one." John's eyes seemed as if they had glazed over and there were dabs of perspiration on his temples.

"Where's the function?" Eva asked.

Dan nodded towards an archway.

"Are you going to be all right Dad?" Eva asked.

"I'm going to be a good boy," he said. "Won't I Dan? Another of these," he handed his empty glass over the bar, "and that'll be me. I'm driving, after all. Isn't that so Dan?"

"Oh yes," agreed his friend, seriously.

"Come on then," Eva said.

I picked up my two glasses and followed her. I found myself in the public bar. It was crowded and smoke-filled.

"What do you think's worse?" asked Eva, turning to me. "Spending the evening watching my father, not an easy task, or letting him get on with it for once, and getting it from Mum later?"

I said, "I'd let him get on with it." I didn't seriously believe this but I knew this was the only way I could get to be alone with her.

We had stopped near a poster and she led me over to it. It was printed on pink day-glow paper and decorated with green shamrocks.

There will be a benefit for the family of Michael O'Flaherty in the Terance MacSwiney room on July 14th starting at 9:00 o'clock sharp. Music by Paddy Brack and Shannon Loch.

"I hope it's good," she said. "It mightn't be but you won't mind, will you?"

"I don't care."

The entrance to the MacSwiney room was blocked by Pat, now in a frilly shirt and a bow tie. The jam-jar of money he was holding looked fragile in his huge hands.

"Carry on," Pat said and stepped aside to let us through.

The MacSwiney room was long and dark. There was a stage at the far end, strewn with musical instruments. On the wall, just inside the entrance where we were standing, was a painting showing the Twelve Pins of Connemara. The mountains were shown as very green and purple, whilst the sky above was very blue but filled with huge swirling clouds like candy floss. The frame was gold.

Eva took me by the arm and brought me over. I saw that it was not a painting but a mural and the frame around it was nailed to the wall. She caught my attention again and smiled at me, raising her eyebrows. There were other paintings in the room, including the Moutains of Mourne and the Giant's Causeway, executed in the same way.

We found a table for ourselves close to the stage and I sat down on a leatherette counter stool which was faintly sticky.

Pat the bouncer was now sitting at a rickety table just inside the doorway. People were filing in and I saw them handing over five-, ten- and twenty-pound notes.

The men who came in were anything between their twenties and their fifties. Their faces looked newly washed and their hair newly combed. They all had big bodies which threatened to break out of the suits which most were wearing.

The women accompanying the men were all wearing dresses which seemed to shimmer faintly in the dimly lighted room. Most of them also wore big gold earrings, necklaces and large bracelets. Sometimes these caught the light and flashed.

A young priest climbed on the stage and went to the microphone.

"Welcome," he said. "I am delighted you could all come. We all know why we are here tonight. Michael O'Flaherty, killed tragically in the course of his work, is what has brought us together: and I know Michael would have been here if it had been any other man. We are a community and this evening we are coming together as a community and demonstrating our solidarity to one another . . ."

As the priest continued I noticed heads turning towards the dark far corner on the other side of the stage. A woman sat there. She had black fluffy hair and red cheeks. She was in her late twenties.

Beside her, there were two boys in blazers with wet hair combed flat and two young girls in white dresses with velvet Alice bands holding their long hair neatly in place. A baby sat on the woman's lap.

"The widow and her children," Eva whispered in my ear.

The priest left the stage to a round of applause and three men who had been standing by one of the speakers jumped up. They all wore identical blue trousers and red shirts with Shannon Loch on the left breast. Two picked up guitars and the third sat behind the drum kit. "Hello," said one of the men; then they all looked at one another, nodded together and started to play an Irish tune at great speed. I looked at Eva's bare crossed legs and saw one foot tapping on the ground.

I went out to buy some more drinks at the bar. When I came back there was an old man standing at our table. He was wearing a dirty red dressing gown tied around the middle with a piece of string and a tightly fitting red woollen hat on his head.

I sat down. He tore a strip of raffle tickets out of a book. Eva took them and handed him a pound. He saluted with two fingers, shouted his thanks above the music to, "M'Lady and his Lordship", and strolled to the next table thumbing his book of tickets like a deck of cards.

"It's fun here," I shouted into her ear.

She picked up the tickets. "First prize is a goose," she shouted back.

A large man bounded on to the stage. As everyone applauded he stood holding the microphone. His face was caught by a spotlight and he looked dazed.

He was wearing a black shirt, with the three top buttons undone so his chest hair and a gold medallion could be seen, black trousers with an immaculate crease down the front, white shoes and a white tuxedo. A red paper napkin was pointing out of the breast pocket. It was more or less the same colour as the carnation in the buttonhole.

The clapping died down. "You can go on if you like," he roared and immediately it started up again. It was Paddy Brack. "Let's h–o–t it up my friends," he shouted, waggling his head and his hands like Al Jolson. "Who says the Irish don't enjoy themselves?"

The audience cheered and the band started "Born in the USA". Within seconds the empty floor was filled with people.

"Let's dance," I said and I steered her by her elbows into the crowd.

We found a space alongside two girls who were jiving together, their pleated skirts rising in the air to reveal clinging white nylon slips beneath. I took Eva's hand and began to turn her. Several couples bumped into us and laughed as they apologised. The feeling on the floor was good humoured. Overhead the mirrored globe slowly turned, casting its silver dappled light on everyone below . . .

Raised voices sounded. Heads swivelled. It was the man in the woollen hat. He was shouting at Pat and waving his arms. Pat was prodding the old man with his finger and shouting back.

Pat turned the old man round and begun to propel him

forward. It was pathetic to see such unmatched opponents. Dancers scattered and the old man shouted incoherently. His red dressing gown floated behind. The music did not stop. In a few seconds it was over.

Paddy Brack finished his song. "Sorry about that folks," he apologised. "Things were a bit hot there for a while but it's all right now."

We went and sat down.

A few minutes later Pat came up and asked if we had any raffle tickets. Eva handed hers over and he gave her her pound back. "The governor's had that old one barred now, so you shouldn't be bothered any more by him. Dirty old tramp," he shouted darkly.

The intermission came. Traditional airs were played over the public address system. A balding man with a wiry, spindle-like body shuffled on to the floor and began to dance a reel, kicking his legs backwards and forwards whilst holding his body stiff and erect.

"Good man Con," several onlookers shouted.

In the second half of the evening, the energetic Con danced by himself, gyrating directly underneath Paddy Brack. He was mesmerising. The top of his bald head grew redder and redder and perspiration started to trickle down his forehead and dripped on to his beard.

Con threw off his jacket and threw it on the stage like a madman issuing a challenge. His white shirt had come out and flapped over the back of his trousers. Although his arms and legs were thin, Con gave an impression of uncontrollable strength when he moved.

The music got faster. Con started to run on the spot while shaking his head from side to side. In the first break between numbers, he clasped Paddy Brack's hands in adoration and looked as though he were on the verge of weeping with emotion. "It's like a religious experience," shouted Eva . . .

Sometime later Con came and asked Eva to dance. She looked at me and I felt good that she should pretend I was her boyfriend.

I nodded.

She followed him out on to the floor. Everyone was jiving but Con put his arms around her and insisted that they waltzed.

When she came back she shouted into my ear, "He asked me if I was married. I said you were my husband."

I felt good again.

A couple of dances later Con came back and asked for another dance. Eva shook her head and he stalked off sullenly. I laid my jacket over the stool and led her out. My head felt numb from the loudness of the music and I had drunk too much. So had she. We danced well and smiled warmly whenever our eyes met.

The lights dimmed and the first of the slow dances began. Without a trace of self-consciousness we put our arms around each other and started to shuffle around the floor. Sometimes her breasts touched against me, sometimes her thighs.

The lights came up and the band started the Irish National Anthem. Everyone assumed a straight face and some sang along. Among the loudest was Con, now in a duffle coat. When it was over, Paddy Brack threw his carnation into the crowd. There was a mad scramble for it. Somehow or other, the elder of the dead man's daughters ended up with it. Her mother pinned it with the Alice band behind the child's ear. The girl's expression was radiant.

We returned to our table. Con was sprawled in a seat nearby. He had a pint of beer in a straight glass which he was drinking greedily. Some of the liquid trickled out of the corner of his mouth and spattered on to his coat. When the glass was empty, Con stood up, burped and lurched off. I felt relieved.

A few minutes later he was back with a drink in each hand.

"I think we should go outside," I whispered to Eva.

"Time please. Time please." Paul, who had stacked the tonic waters, was sweeping through the room, emptying ashtrays, wiping tables and putting glasses into a plastic basin.

"Fuck off!" shouted Con.

"Time please, ladies and gentlemen. You must go home to your beds."

". . . And fuck off you and your stuck-up bitch," continued Con.

It was not Paul who was being addressed, I now realised, but myself and Eva.

"Yes, fuck off, you cunt and your stuck-up bitch."

Con lashed out with his foot. He caught the table at which we were sitting on the underneath. It went up in the air taking all the glasses with it. For a moment everything seemed to stand still, then there was a terrible crash as the lot hit the ground. Eva cried out and I stood up with my heart racing.

"Now why did you do that?" asked Paul, from the next table. His tone was good humoured.

Con looked around.

"Wasn't that a daft thing to do?"

Con let out a roar and sprang at Paul. The basin with the glasses tumbled to the floor. Someone shouted, "Get Pat, quick."

Paul was on his back and Con was starting to pummel him on the face.

I ran forward, grabbed the hood of the duffle coat and began to tug. The drummer from the Shannon Loch took hold of the assailant's flailing arms.

"Move aside," I heard and I felt myself being pulled away. It was Pat. Effortlessly, he hoisted Con up and began to frogmarch him towards the exit. Cries of "Cunt" and "Bastard" echoed round the MacSwiney room. "I'll sue" was the last we heard and then Con was gone.

I started picking up the few glasses which had rolled away unbroken and putting them in a basin. Eva came over.

"That was very brave," she said.

In the scuffle Con had caught me and there was a dirt-mark on my cheek she told me. She put saliva on the end of her thumb and wiped it off.

We went through to the saloon. Dan was standing in front of the bar with his hands in his pockets, my father beside him. John's face was flushed and his hair looked as if it were damp with sweat. He'd been drinking.

Dan apologised for what he called "the fracas" and ordered double-brandies for each of us. It was Pat who served them from behind the bar. His chest was like a barrel. As he pushed the drinks across the wood, I saw his forearms were as thick as the plough's handles.

After closing time the doors were locked. No-one was asked to leave.

"Who was that man in the red dressing gown?" Eva asked.

"We call him the Tea Cosy. He's a trouble maker," said Dan. "He comes in here of a night and sells raffle tickets but he keeps the money. You see there's no draw at all. He's a swindler. I don't mind him making a few quid in the public bar or the saloon but in there . . ." Dan waved towards the MacSwiney room. ". . . it was a benefit tonight and that wasn't right what he did. We were going to have a raffle ourselves, with all the proceeds going to the family you see, only the Tea Cosy buggered it up. So I've had him barred. He can spend all his nights under the railway arches from now on for all I care. And he won't find another pub in West London that'll have him."

Eva looked anxious.

"Does he sleep rough?" she asked.

"Anywhere he can. And he's welcome to. I've had him barred for life. He won't come in here again, will he Pat?"

"No," said Pat, delicately drying a glass in his huge hands.

Dan let us out by the side door and bolted it after us. In the alley stood a woman with her dress hoisted to show off her knees. The car park was empty except for my father's Sierra. Those who stayed late to drink must have gone home on foot.

"You're not driving Dad," said Eva.

She fished in the pocket of John's suit jacket and took out the keys. She gave them to me. They were on a ring along with a *Playboy* medallion.

"I'm quite all right. I can drive," John said firmly.

"But I'd be happy to," I replied.

I opened the front door on the passenger side after a little difficulty with the key. This was only the third or fourth time I'd driven the Sierra.

"I'm not going to argue," said my father across the car roof.

He came around and lowered himself down and into the seat. His movements were slow, as if he were stunned slightly, and his face was puffed up and white.

Eva got into the back and I nosed the car into the alley. The woman showing her knees was still standing where we had left her. She stared at us as we passed.

We turned into the street. It was filled with empty, brightly lit shops. At the first red traffic light I saw the Tea Cosy. He was standing in a shop doorway with refrigerators in the windows around him.

"Look," I said.

"Hang on," she replied.

I could hear her rooting in her purse.

She jumped out, ran over to the Tea Cosy, and emptied out all her change into his hand.

The lights went to green.

The car behind us honked.

Eva started to run towards us.

"A soft touch," her father said, "but a very good girl."

I looked at her brown, faintly bandy legs, her small breasts, her large head, and felt slightly funny.

She sprang into the back of the car and we drove away.

"When Eva was a child, we used to catch her sometimes leaving money in the street, *on* the pavement."

John, with his head on the back of the seat, was looking towards me.

"I said to her, or Teresa said to her one day, 'What do you do that for?' and she said, 'I'm putting it there for the people who are hungry so they can buy themselves something to eat.'"

"Dad don't tell embarrassing stories about me."

John rolled his head from side to side. The smell of brandy wafted from him.

"A soft touch but a very good girl," he whispered. A moment later he was asleep and snoring quietly.

"What's your mother going to say?" I was driving very slowly and very carefully, with my eyes fixed intently on the road.

"She is not going to be pleased," Eva said. She continued in a mock Hungarian accent, "Why didn't you stop him?" and then went on, in her own voice, "Because, Mum, I was out for the evening with Malachy and I didn't want to spend it watching Dad."

"Anyway," I said, "you know what would have happened if you had?"

"I suppose so."

"It wouldn't have made a blind bit of difference."

"I suppose you're right," she said slowly. After a moment she added, "Yes, you are", very brightly and gave me a warm squeeze on the back of my neck while her father snored on beside us.

John

John O'Neill was born in 1941. His elder brother Peter was nineteen and away studying engineering. His two sisters were boarding at their convent. When they completed their Leaving Certificates, they went to Dublin to train as secretaries. John's childhood in effect was like that of an only child. He slept alone. He played alone. He went to school alone.

The atmosphere in the house was oppressive. When his father was sober his parents rarely spoke except to exchange platitudes about the weather or the food they were eating or the price of farm animals. When his father was drunk they only shouted at one another. Walter would hit his wife and sometimes he would hit John as well. This was particularly when the young lad annoyed him by crying.

Once his father got a gun and threatened to shoot them both and they went and hid for the night in the barn. It was all a joke Walter explained to them later. There had been no ammunition in the chamber.

Another time he brought a pickaxe into the house with the intention of splitting Margaret in two and splattering her brains around the kitchen floor. John threw salt in his father's face and fled with his mother to the safety of Dr Quinn's.

Overcome by remorse on account of his attempted murder (the pickaxe was no joke) Walter disappeared on a spree. It was a month before he was located by the Garda, in a small hotel in Ennis. He was suffering from delirium tremens.

He was brought home very sick. He was thin like a bird and an ulcer had been diagnosed. The doctor recommended a regime of recuperation. Walter was to stay in bed and he was to be treated as an invalid.

John had been four at the time of the gun incident and he hadn't quite grasped what had been going on. He was ten now and he understood better.

While his mother sat with his father for long hours in Walter's bedroom, spoon feeding him chicken broth and little squares of white toast without crusts, John would creep out of the house. Sometimes he would roam the fields but usually he would go and sit in the middle of the rhododendron bush and brood.

Why his mother had married was what puzzled him. Walter was so obviously unsuitable. This in turn led to the question, Why was his father the way that he was? There were plenty of other fathers in the parish who drank. Who drank so much they would get into fights or fall down in the street. But Walter was not like them. He was in a league of his own. They knew it in the family and John was certain everyone else in the parish sensed it too. When Walter drank Walter was a killer.

This conclusion only returned John to his starting point. Why had his mother married? Their first encounter, when Walter had driven her home in his lorry, stopping at every pub along the route and leaving her alone in the cab while he went in for a drink, was already known to John. It was one of Walter's favourite stories. His father's drinking was clearly known to Margaret from the outset. Yet still she had married him.

The past was a mystery which he couldn't fathom. Maybe, he thought, the explanation was that his parents had been "in love" which, as he understood it, was what people were before they got married and then subsequently this had stopped. They certainly weren't in love any more. He could be certain of that. They didn't hold hands and they never linked arms in the street as married couples round about the parish did. So why did his mother remain, he wondered, if there was no longer love to keep her at home? Why didn't they just leave, him and her, taking with them only a few possessions, and roam the roads, sleeping in ditches and begging for food? Nothing could be worse than their present existence.

One day, sitting in the rhododendron bush, he saw the answer with terrible clarity. She didn't love him. That's why she stayed. She didn't love him enough to go into the world with him. She was punishing him by making him stay, and the reason obviously she was doing that was because there was something the matter with him.

It wasn't logical but it was all he could come up with to explain his circumstances.

Having reached this terrible conclusion, he now strove to make his mother change her mind. He excelled at school. He was always offering to help around the house or to fetch messages from the village. He was endlessly polite.

This had the effect on Margaret of increasing her love into something near infatuation. Here was a son who treated her with all the attentiveness of a husband and a lover. Here, from her own son, was what she had deserved all her life from her husband but never received. Her feelings, as she showed them to her son, seemed a little like worship.

John accepted this but in his heart he didn't believe she meant it. It was a front. He still believed what he had seen in the rhododendron bushes. There was something the matter with him and his mother was simply trying to make him think she hadn't seen or didn't care.

When he was seventeen John took his first drink. He got very drunk and was sick but went on drinking. He found the feeling of intoxication absolutely magnificent.

When he woke up the next morning, he saw finally how everything fitted into place.

His mother hadn't loved him and indeed couldn't love him for a simple reason. Like his father, he was a drunk.

The very next year he went to Manchester, New Jersey.

In America John drank heavily. He married Amy and went on drinking although he pretended to his new wife that he wasn't. He was drunk when he met Ailish, the young girl from Tuam who became his mistress. He got drunk when he heard she had been picked up by the Immigration authorities and was to be deported, and learnt what Amy's part in this had been. After a week he sobered up and was overcome by a cold and ruthless sense of self-preservation. He got through the divorce without drinking and left the country. Travelling to Europe on the boat was the next occasion on which he drank. After twenty-four hours he sobered up and his innate sense of self-preservation returned to command again. This was the pattern which he followed for the rest of his life: binges alternating with periods of sobriety, just like his father before him.

Diary, Hampton Wick

John was asleep when we got home, his head leaning against the glass of the window. I pulled up near the front door and turned off the key in the ignition. We sat in the car without speaking for a while and then I said,

"We might get him upstairs without Teresa hearing."

"I doubt it," Eva whispered back. "She's probably at the top of the stairs even now, with the rolling pin under her arm." Eva switched to her Hungarian accent. "In bloody Irish pub they make him drink too much as usual, and you don't bloody stop him. What do you bloody think I sent you along for?"

We laughed together quietly then she leant forward in her seat and shook her father by the shoulder.

"Dad, wake up."

He cleared his throat and I could smell his brandy breath again.

"Come on dearie," she said.

Eva got out and took the handle of the front passenger door. As it opened her father tumbled sideways and she caught his head with both hands.

"Where am I?" he asked.

"Where do you think?"

"James, that's my front door isn't it?" he slurred in a mock upper-class English accent.

He had got out and was on his feet.

"Carry on James," John continued, pretending to throw a coin to Eva, and he started forward, moving unsteadily.

With gravel sounding beneath his feet, John started to declaim:

'Twas down the glen one Easter morn
To a city fair rode I

When Ireland's lines of marching men
In squadrons passed me by,

and then half-singing he continued:

No pipe did hum and no battle drum
Did sound its dread tattoo
But the Angelus bell o'er the Liffey's swell
Rang out in the foggy dew.

"Dad," hissed Eva, "it's two o'clock in the morning." She was on the front step sliding in the Yale.

I locked the Sierra's doors and came up behind the two of them. She pushed the door and it glided backwards, the light from the street lamp by the gate glistening in the glass panes.

"No-one about," I said.

The hall light clicked on and there at the top of the stairs was Teresa. Her hair was tied back in a severe pony tail and she was wearing her pink flannel dressing gown.

"Hello," she said very coldly.

"'llo there," John called back sweetly and with extraordinary alacrity he shot down the hall and disappeared into the kitchen. I heard the noise of the neon light coming on and then a tap running.

"Good evening?" asked Teresa.

"Very fine," Eva replied and closed the door behind us.

"I enjoyed it very much," I added.

"Give John a couple of Panadol and point him towards the stairs," said Teresa.

She padded away across the landing and disappeared into her bedroom.

"Oh-oh," Eva said.

"She's not very pleased."

"I'm in for the long looks tomorrow."

Entering the kitchen, I heard the sound of retching. In the utility room, which was next door, John was vomiting over the butler sink. He had heard us coming and with a leg shut the door. Eva turned on the kettle and with a rumble it came to life.

"What a way to finish the evening!"

"I thought it was pretty perfect," I said, "and this doesn't matter at all."

Cupping her hands around the kettle she turned her head and looked at me. The strength of affection was unmistakable, like warmth from a fire. She held her gaze for a long time, before finally turning away and reaching down the tea caddy from the cupboard.

The door from the utility room opened. John's face was pale white whilst his eyes seemed to shine a bright blue. He was holding the orange basin in which he had caught his sick. There was the acid smell of vomit mixed with brandy.

Eva opened the kitchen door and then the sliding doors of the veranda beyond. John carried the basin past the ping-pong table and out into the garden. Eva handed me a cup of tea. I took a small sip and watched his dark figure going to the compost heap at the very bottom of the garden and tipping the basin there.

"Sorry about that folks," he said when he came back. He rinsed his basin and his hands in the sink and went through the door saying, "Good night."

Eva put her cup down and followed him out. I heard her muttering something to him in the hall and then the sound of their footsteps as they climbed the stairs.

I turned on the radio. I could find nothing among the crackles but a station playing "Lover's Rock". I set the volume level and sat down at the kitchen table. I began to follow the melody line of the song and was soon vaguely hypnotised. I forgot about the numbness in my ears and how I felt. My mind became first still and later empty; and then into it slid the memory of the very first time I had come to Hampton Wick . . .

I saw myself ringing the bell and then waiting. I was staring at the glass panes in the front door, the palms trees etched in them, trying to catch a glimpse of a blurred movement inside, and straining my ears for the sound of footfalls.

I heard someone behind me saying, "Hello." The word was spoken quietly, a little hesitantly, as if the speaker had determined to speak in a low tone in order that I shouldn't be given a fright.

I turned round and saw a broad face, a nice broad face with high cheekbones and shoulder-length reddish hair. There was a fraction of an instant as I recognised this was a girl and then shock. It was as if some special force was pushing from all directions on some special place in the middle of my body. I had felt something like this once or twice before, when I had met girls for the first time with whom I had subsequently had affairs, but this was the first occasion I had this feeling as strongly. It was love – I was certain of that – because I was filled with the certain sense that here was the person I had been waiting all my life to meet, the person who was the other half of myself.

She took a couple of steps towards me. She moved slowly, taking little sharp intakes of breath as if she were in pain. I looked down and saw the ground where we were standing was gravelled and her feet were bare . . .

On the radio a voice spoke. The memory vanished like a fish in the sea when it's been disturbed. The disc jockey was reading a dedication to a group called the Brent Posse. There were footsteps overhead and someone was talking loudly. I couldn't tell who but assumed it was Teresa. Another slow, mesmeric song started. I poured myself a whisky, drank it down in one, and then took a second, a third and a fourth. I wanted to go back to the memory of the first time I had visited the house but the liquor wouldn't help me. I couldn't get back to the distant past. Instead I found myself following the singer on the radio, crooning about her Daddy-oh and how she was goin' to be good to him, and then floating back to a few hours earlier . . .

Propelling Eva on to the dance floor at the start of the evening, I was unable to stop myself looking down her body to her legs. She was wearing a black dress and plain black pumps. The skin of her calves looked faintly red in the dimly lit interior of the MacSwiney room. As we danced, I found myself not looking at the other dancers, as I usually do, but down at her and straight into her eyes. She looked straight back up at me. She was doing as I was doing. I was certain she felt as I felt.

This was new. There had been no element of desire before. The first time I had set eyes on Eva, I had simply felt that I had at long last found what I had always been missing.

In the weeks which followed my move into the house, there was no desire either. I had felt it was enough to be near her and I had felt grateful we were becoming friends.

I had imagined this was how our summer would continue and then came the evening in The Plough . . .

By the time I led Eva on to the floor the second time, we'd both had too much to drink, and we were both stunned by having been in a room for too long where the music was too loud.

The slow music started. We put our arms around one another and started to shuffle around the floor. Every now and again a leg touched or a breast brushed, and I felt a sense of excitement behind the groin where it always starts.

I felt it again watching Eva as she ran towards the car after she had given the tramp in the High Street all her money . . .

The feeling was still with me when she returned to the kitchen. She poured herself a drink and sat down. I stared across the table at her. I reached over and gave her hand a squeeze. She must have stood up because suddenly she was standing over me. As she leant forward I felt her hair brushing my cheeks. Our lips touched. We kissed. First with our mouths closed, then open. Our tongues touched, gently at first and then with more force. I pulled her down on to my lap. I felt her arms around my neck and put my arms around her. Her breasts pressed against me. In that place in the body where desire gathers, I could feel it collecting. On the radio the voice of the singer trilled and swooped. The doors were still open to the garden and a cold breeze crept in bringing with it the smell of roses. Suddenly a picture leapt into my thoughts. I saw us from above, as if I were a balloon floating near the ceiling and looking down, . . . I and her; her brown legs; her black dress most of the way up her thighs. It's not right, said an inner voice – it sounded cool and detached – or perhaps I even said this out loud, and the next moment she climbed from my lap and glided away, calling, "Good night", from the doorway before she disappeared.

I closed the doors to the garden and drank more whisky. Her footfalls sounded above and the pipes in the bathroom clattered as she ran the tap. I presumed she was washing her teeth. The drain outside the kitchen window gurgled.

After a decent interval had elapsed, I found my own way upstairs, unsteadily. I had drunk too much. I washed my own teeth briefly, the bathroom floor swaying around my feet, slipped past the door beyond which my half-brother was sleeping soundly, and fell into bed. The room wheeled around me and I closed my eyes. Before I could do anything to stop it, it was there again, Eva's face as I had seen it that very first time, peering round the side of the house. Then in my mind's eye I saw her whole body as she took those two steps forward, before she turned to lead me to the family in the garden . . .

Two cracked halves of a plate which together made a whole . . .

Half-awake, half-asleep, I saw Eva's face melt into a naked female torso which was a face; the nipples the eyes, the sex the mouth.

Pressing with my front on to the mattress my semen trickled out. Moments later, drifting towards sleep, I could feel it drying and crinkling my skin.

The next morning I woke up to find the house empty. Everyone had gone to their work; Malachy to Heathrow and Montgomery Meats; John into town to one of his businesses; Teresa to the Social Services department in Merton; and Eva to Price's Late-nite Chemist.

The moment I opened my eyes I felt overwhelmed by a great wave of anxiety. In my mind's eye I saw myself with Eva sitting on my lap and winced. It was obvious what I had to do. I had to leave immediately.

I piled all my clothes into my large blue holdall. I did this hurriedly. I was panic-stricken.

I noticed I was short of some socks and a fluffy cotton shirt. I had bought this on my first trip to Niagara Falls aged sixteen and I was very attached to it. I found my things in the basket in the laundry room, and wrapped them up in a plastic bag.

From the hall I telephoned the Cumberland Hotel. I reserved a room.

Climbing the stairs of the Hampton Wick house I could hear my footsteps booming although I was walking on the carpet. When I did up the zip on my holdall the noise sounded thunderous. Closing the bedroom door after myself, I could hear the catch clicking in the silence.

In the kitchen I found the notepad used for leaving messages.

At the top of the page was printed *O'Neill's Tarmacadaming Services.*

I sat down at the table and wrote:

> Thank you all. I haven't gone far. Only to the hotel where I was staying before. The best way I can say what I want to say is with a Spanish proverb: Three days to stay is enough, otherwise the guest starts to stink like a fish. I know we shall get together before I go home. I shall search London for a suitable restaurant and take you all out to dinner. Thank you a millionfold for your hospitality.

I finished the letter *With all my love* and signed my name. I propped it against the butter dish.

I carried my bags through the front door and closed it. My heart was racing. I took the keys which Teresa had given me out of my pocket. After this, there would be no going back.

I lifted up the flap and popped the keys through. They dropped with a dull noise on to the mat inside. I picked up my bags and quickly began to walk.

At the station I bought my ticket. I went and stood on the platform. I was struck then by a horrible thought. Supposing, for some reason, some member of the family had to come back that morning, and coming in on the 'down' train from London, they got out and saw me standing on the opposite platform, with my bags, waiting for the 'up' train?

There was no waiting room and there was nothing to hide behind, so I took my bags and went half-way down the steps which led to the ticket office and eventually the street below. It was a dark, dank place with slogans on the brick walls, and passersby looked at me standing there with curiosity. The 'down' train came first and then my own. I went up and got on.

It pulled out of the station. Outside the grimy window the leafy suburbs slipped by. For most of the journey which followed I was in a state of trance. I didn't either notice what was going on or think about what I was doing. It was not until we rattled on to the bridge which spanned the Thames that I started looking around myself.

The tide was out. On the black mud, boats lay beached, tilting at extraordinary angles. One or two abandoned vessels had sunk right in and their rotting hulls resembled to me, at that moment, the human ribcage. It occurred to me then I had just made the most awful mistake.

What was I running away from? For one of the most stupid reasons imaginable. I hadn't done anything. I had turned tail because of what I felt. I was frightened of it. That was no reason.

I think this is what I thought as the river slid below me. I know with absolute certainty that I was also feeling bereft; the same way I had felt when our parents left us at home as children to go to a party – and the same way as when, later, I had gone away, first to summer camp and then to the small apartment which I rented when I first left home.

I felt a great surge of pain and hurt at the back of my throat. I immediately began to feel angry with myself. I wanted to hit my chin with my own fist and feel my own hot tears on my cheeks.

The train pulled into Waterloo and this self-indulgence was cut short.

I got out and carried my luggage to one of the plastic seats and sat down. What would my father say about this, I wondered? "What have we done?" came the answer almost immediately. But what about the humiliation, I wondered, of having done something so stupid and having to own up to it?

In my mind's eye appeared my stupid letter, tilted against the butter dish.

I found a telephone and dropped a tenpenny coin into the slot.

999 calls only, came up the message in the window above the buttons.

I looked at my watch. Three minutes before the next train left.

At the next telephone the coin just kept clattering through and ending up in the return slot.

At the third telephone, the message lit up in the window, *10p credit*. I dialled. At the other end the O'Neills' 'phone rang. Come on, come on, I thought, pick up the 'phone. As soon as I heard "Hello" I knew just what I was going to say: "Look, I've made a terrible mistake. Forget the letter. I'm coming back."

I looked at my watch. A minute to go. The dialling tone gave way to a crackling line and my heart sank. "Hello, you've just got through to . . ." The ansaphone was on.

I banged the receiver down and started running for the gate. Two or three men ahead of me were also running.

The guard clipped my ticket and I was on to the platform. I only had to get to the last carriage, fumble with the door and get in.

"Hello, fancy seeing you again . . .

". . . Don't you remember me?" the thin piping voice continued from behind. "I remember you . . ."

Half-way along the platform the guard raised his flag. I could hear the rush of air which signalled the automatic doors were about to close.

". . . You're in a rush . . ." said the voice behind.

I skipped through and the whistle sounded. I held something to steady myself and the train moved off. The train spotter slid past the window. His arm was raised and I waved back. He shouted something but I couldn't hear what he said.

I found a seat and I spent the rest of the journey raging at myself for what I had done, or being overwhelmed by great rushes of frustrated fury at the inordinate length of time the train seemed to spend at each station.

Pulling into Hampton Wick, I was standing ready by the door. As soon as the train stopped, I was down and off.

In the street outside I started at a half-run. The bags banged against my legs. My forehead started to sweat and one or two beads trickled into my eyes, making them smart. Between my lungs, I began to feel a sharp, stabbing pain.

I reached the house and went straight to the front door. I had my sentence ready, "I'm sorry. Forget the letter. I made a terrible mistake."

I pressed the white bell button. Nothing. That meant that no-one had read the letter – which was good. But before I had time to enjoy any sense of relief, there was a new horror.

It was a picture of myself on the gravel, the bags beside me, and Eva or Teresa or Malachy or John, standing at the gate and looking at me.

How was I going to get in before anyone came back? I remembered Henry and Paul next door. They had a key.

I hid my bags under the hedge and ran round.

Henry answered the door.

"I've locked myself out. Could I borrow the key?"

Henry was in his thirties. He had dark hair and a dark moustache. He wore shorts and a running singlet which showed off his muscular shoulders.

"Who are you?"

"I'm staying next door."

"Oh yes, you're staying with Teresa and John. Come in. I won't be a mo. I've just got to turn off the sprinkler. Make yourself comfy in the lounge."

"Could I have the key now? I'm in a bit of a rush."

"I've got to find it first," he said from the end of the hall then turned on his bare legs and disappeared into the kitchen.

I wandered through to the lounge, hoping I could hate it. The carpet was dove grey; the sofas were covered with fake pink velvet; on the walls there were four enormous water-colours of David Bowie dressed and made-up as Ziggy Stardust. Each was signed in huge, rounded handwriting, *To the boys (Henry & Paul) from Pete the Meat.* I was delighted they were so awful.

I sat down. The sofas were filled with dense, unyielding foam. It was rather like sitting on a pumice stone. This I could not wait to put in my diary.

Then I remembered that for at least thirty seconds I hadn't thought about the letter or what I'd done. My vindictive feelings suddenly lost their magic and my heart started to race again.

Henry reappeared.

"Let's see," he said.

From the cigar box he was holding he extracted a cardboard tag with Teresa's distinctive writing on it. The keys dangled below.

"Thank you so much," I said but before I could get them from him he replied, "I'll come with you. I've got to go down to the shops anyway. Save you bringing them back."

"I'm happy to bring them back."

"I'd be going anyway. I'll just get my shopper."

Waiting in the hall I imagined what I'd like to say to him. "With do-gooders like you around it's hardly surprising the world's in a mess." Or, "Just give me the key and piss off back to your garden." Or finally, plain and to the point, "You are a cretin."

He emerged from the kitchen. His sandals creaked. Behind he trundled a tartan-covered shopping trolley.

"Just got to turn on the burglar alarm."

"I am in a bit of a hurry."

"It only takes a second and it's worth it for all the trouble and pain it could save later on."

He opened the cupboard under the stairs, pressed buttons on a box and turned a key. The alarm started.

"We've got ten seconds," he said.

I got out the front door and started going for the gate. I hate it when people are in a hurry and walk ahead to gee me up, so I suppose it was as much to irritate him as because I was impatient that I did this. The door shut behind me and the burglar alarm stopped.

"Just got to double-lock," he called after my back, still sounding mild and friendly.

"Sprinkler off?" I asked.

"Yes."

He was uncertain how to judge my tone.

"Haven't left the iron on have we?"

"No."

"All the plugs pulled out, I trust?"

He walked up to me and stared into my eyes.

"You're a bit of a card, aren't you?"

"We did remember the shopping list, I hope."

We turned and started to walk slowly, and in silence, the little wheels on the basket rumbling behind.

We reached the O'Neills' front door.

Henry put his hands into his pockets.

"Oh dear. I've forgotten the keys."

Malachy, don't say a thing, don't look at him, I thought.

I stared at the palm trees etched into the opaque panes of glass set in the front door.

"April Fool."

He rattled the keys coyly in my ear.

"Funny. Very funny," I said.

"Oh dear, no more humour."

I thought, I'm going to fucking hit him if he doesn't get that door open.

"Is there a dead lock?"

"Yes."

"How did you lock yourself out with the dead lock on?"

He inserted the mortis key and turned it.

"It's a long story."

"I bet it is."

He slid in the Yale key. The door opened and then immediately caught at the bottom on the keys I had posted through. He picked them up.

"My keys. Thank you very much."

"Any time."

He sauntered off, turned through the gate on to the pavement, and gave me a little wave across the hedge.

"Any time," he called and disappeared from sight.

I rushed in and got the letter. I took it into the garden and burnt it on top of the compost heap. Then I buried the charred pieces under the mouldering cuttings.

I felt such a sense of relief, I lay down on the lawn.

There was a lid of grey sky overhead with dimples in it. The sun beating behind had warmed up the air. There was a smell of grass and the buzzing of bees somewhere.

I fell into a deep sleep and woke I don't know how much later.

I lay still and thought about the events of the morning; hiding in the station; cursing myself on the train; waiting for Henry to find the key.

I started to laugh quietly and then I remembered.

I sat up. My heart started beating; sweat appeared instantly on my palms; I felt sick. It was no wonder the perfect murder was so hard to pull off. There were so many things to think about.

I raced through the house and opened the front door. At just that moment Eva turned through the front gate. Glancing to my left, I could clearly see my bags under the privet. What if Eva should see them? How would I explain? Happily, the night before didn't enter my thoughts. All my anxiety was focused under the hedge.

"Hello," she called. "Are you going out?"

"No. Yes. Well I was. Why aren't you at work?"

"I get the morning off."

She was wearing a felt hat with a wide brim which flopped as she moved. It seemed a very odd addition to the plain yellow dress she was wearing.

"Do you like it?" she asked, pulling the hat further down on to her head. "Tenpence in the Sue Ryder shop. I know a bargain when I see one."

"Very nice."

Please let her come in and please let me get my luggage, I prayed. My heart was thumping but at least the hurdle of how to start talking after what had happened the night before was cleared. In a sense, these were the best circumstances under which to meet, gripped by a panic which blotted all other worries out.

"What do you think of this?"

Out of a crumpled plastic bag she pulled a purple kaftan. The embroidery on the front was inlaid with slivers of mirror.

"Lovely isn't it?"

"Yes."

"You don't like it?"

"Yes I do."

"No you don't."

I went back to the hall and she followed. I closed the door very smartly behind her. My haste was a little suspicious but I don't think she noticed.

We went into the kitchen and I turned on the kettle. The shadow of the evening before had just appeared.

"I think I'll try this on."

She changed into the kaftan in the utility room.

She came out. The kaftan was full length, with a slit at each side which went as far as the thigh. The fabric puffed forward around the breast in an ugly way.

"What do you think?"

It was horrible. This was self-abasement although of a strain so mild only someone who was in love would have noticed.

"I like it very much," I lied.

I was being allowed a privileged glimpse of the dark side of my idol. Besides not liking this, I was also frightened. When we see the cracks in another, our first thought is our own jeopardy, not theirs.

"You don't really like it," she said.

I am a bad liar and she had seen through me. Under other circumstances (for instance if this had been my mother) I think I'd have given up but here I didn't.

"No," I continued, determined to brazen it out. "I really do like it. What you need are seven veils and an ankle bracelet and you'll be a picture."

She laughed and I knew that for the first time that summer I had fallen in her estimation.

"I'm sorry about what happened last night," I said.

"I've forgotten about it."

"I didn't mean to embarrass you."

"You didn't embarrass me."

"You're being very nice about it."

"I'm not."

"I'm sure I did embarrass you."

"We both embarrassed one another," she said coldly.

Over coffee I asked, "Why do you get so blue?" (Imagining blue struck just the right note of informality.)

"I thought that was a kind of music," she said (it was a terrible joke) in a tone which was a measure of how far something had changed between us in the course of a night's sleep.

"OK, sad," I said testily. I wasn't so nice either. I might have dropped in her estimation but she'd gone down in mine too.

"I've no intention of answering such a personal question . . ."

I went on asking anyway, in such a way as was guaranteed to make her like me less; and she parried in such a way I also had no choice but to like her less. It was the subtlest demolition of a relationship I'd ever witnessed, and also the most bizarre since it needed both of us working together to bring it about. One dissenting remark, one "What are we doing this for?" and I think the whole scene would have collapsed but neither of us said such a thing. We stuck to our parts, the dialogue rattled on like clock-work, and with one part of my intelligence I watched it, absolutely amazed, open-mouthed. Now of course I understand; it was the taboo swinging into operation.

The conversation wound to a close. Eva stood up.

"I think," she said, "all the bad which has happened stays in the blood."

It was not a concept which I'd ever thought about but she didn't wait for me to answer. Leaving me to choke on what she thought was her best, barbed exit line (and which I now see as the key to everything) she went upstairs to run herself a bath. After the metaphorical bloodletting, it was necessary to wash, I supposed. After she had been in the bath a few minutes, I shouted a bogus question through the door and from her answer gathered she was lying in the water. It was safe to carry out the remaining task.

I spirited my luggage up the stairs and back to my room, where the whole fiasco had started a few hours before. I unpacked. I even went to the trouble of returning the shirt and the socks to the basket by the washing machine from where I had earlier retrieved them.

Diary, Donegal

We were in Ireland . . .

I turned my back on the village shop and started to cycle away. It was a small, ragged road, full of holes, with scatterings of gravel lying here and there. As the tyres crunched over them, an eerie ping would sometimes sound in the inner tubes. I passed the National school, and one or two houses, and then the hill started in earnest. It wasn't long before I was puffed out. The old bicycle was heavy and it was made heavier by the groceries. These were piled in the swaying, creaking front basket, tied with string to the handlebars owing to how the leather straps had long since perished.

I dismounted and started to push. The reassuring tick-tick-tick of the chain started. The side of the road was bounded by grassy banks, gorse bushes with their small yellow flowers, and copses of fir and pine trees which enclosed a shadowy and mysterious world. Further up, the land fell away on one side and in the bottom of the valley below stood a few houses with slate roofs and nearly blue smoke curling from the chimneys, and a river which wound its way sluggishly along.

Somewhere a lark started trilling and I looked about for it in an idle way. It was a warm July day with swollen white clouds everywhere which appeared never to move, and which reminded me of "Galleons Becalmed", a picture I remembered from some childhood book whose name I had long forgotten. The backdrop of sky beyond them was a washed, pale blue. This was only right I thought, as I searched unsuccessfully for the tell-tale black dot of the bird. That morning it had rained, like it had every morning we had been in Donegal. This had cleaned the sky. Then had come the afternoon which, like its predecessors, was a glory.

The crest of the hill came and the road levelled out. I stopped to look over a gate into a field filled with sheep, their fleeces newly shorn, nibbling at the grass.

Beyond the animals, hills rolled towards the horizon. On their lower reaches they were a patchwork of different shades of green – I had never thought there could be so many – separated by ragged hedgerows, while at the top they were all bog, open, undivided and a deep brown colour.

I listened to the sheep bleating quietly and the clacking made by their teeth as they ate. In the distance the lark still trilled and sang.

Then our return entered my thoughts. We'd arrived on Friday for the long weekend which Eva and Malachy had been promising me almost since I'd started staying at their house in Hampton Wick. Today was Monday. The next day was the day we would leave. In my mind's eye I saw the motorway leading south from Liverpool, stretching ahead of the car windscreen, mile after mile of it, the tame English countryside alternating with chimneys and factories, city suburbs and their houses with their grey and red roofs spreading away like a sea.

On the outskirts of London, where the houses crowded up to the side of the road, a faint sense of depression would set in and forgotten preoccupations would start to nag; letters that had to be written; shoes that had to be brought to the mender's; promises made but not acted upon.

At the brow of the hill I turned into our lane. It was deeply pitted and rutted. The bicycle rose and fell like something at sea as I pushed it along. I put one hand on the basket to stop the tins of pineapple chunks bumping out.

Half-way along there was a small grey cottage with dark blue doors and windows. Walter lived here; John had settled it on his father after Margaret's death, which had left him, just one old man alone, rattling around the gloomy family house outside Church Hill.

"Walter," I called and the door opened and he came out.

For a man who had abused his body his entire life, Walter had survived remarkably. He was thin, his face was red and he suffered from a slight stoop. Yet his eyes were bright and he moved with great agility and energy. He put his longevity down to the fact that he still had a few cows and having to water them and to feed them every day involved him in a lengthy walk, and to the fact that he had two acres at the back which he cultivated himself. My half-brother Malachy had a different view. "He lives off pure spite, he thrives on it," he had whispered in my ear after we had been first introduced. I took the diplomatic position and wondered if it wasn't a mixture of exercise and the animosities which were clearly still bubbling in him that kept him alive and alert. Sometimes, I gathered, he still went on the occasional drinking spree.

"Here you are."

I held out the *Irish Independent* which Walter had asked me to buy for him in the village shop. He took it with emaciated fingers and folded it under his arm.

"Nice day," I volunteered.

"Not bad. The glass says rain though."

He was turning to go.

"Oh, I forgot," I called after him.

I took out of my pocket the change from the pound note he had given me to buy the paper.

When he saw it he said "Ahh", and went on turning away. I would not have been surprised to hear him say, Buy yourself an ice cream.

He was in a hurry to get inside with his paper. "Thanks, see you later," he called and the door banged shut.

I went on down the lane, turned the corner and there was the house. John had bought it and the cottage where his father was at the same time, the idea being that Walter would keep an eye on everything.

It was a two-storey, stone dwelling, neither special nor ugly. It had once been the home of the teacher who had taught John's mother, for this was Margaret's village. After he had bought the house, John's original intention had been to pull it down and to put up a bungalow but Teresa wouldn't let him. Having been thwarted in his desire to have something modern, John's next plan was to tinker with the house until it looked modern. What he had in mind was a coat of pebble-dash, metal-framed windows instead of the old sash ones, and a fake Georgian doorway with a fanlight and hollow, fibre-glass pillars instead of the plain oak door. Teresa wouldn't let him do any of this either. This left the house as it was, plain, unpretentious, grey and a little dour.

Eva and her friend Avril, who had come to Ireland as well, were in the garden at the side. They were sitting on deck chairs drinking bottles of Guinness. I leant the bicycle against the wall near the kitchen door and heard Avril calling, "Hey, come and have a drink."

"OK," I said.

"You don't sound very enthusiastic."

Avril, who had been trying to please me since we had set out on Thursday afternoon, had precisely the opposite effect with everything she did from the one she intended. From the start her overt friendliness had irritated me. Yet the more off-hand I had become, the greater were the efforts Avril had made, and was continuing to make.

I walked across the grass. Avril, obliging as always, had gone to the shed to fetch another deck chair and was setting it up for me. She was putting it opposite her, and next to Eva.

Avril's hair was long and hennaed red. She wore an old-fashioned bathing costume, with a red fringed skirt and ruche around her heavy breasts. The colour accentuated the whiteness of her body. Her eyes were grey and the most prominent feature of her face was her large, slightly crooked nose.

"Thanks," I said and sat down on the deck chair. The canvas was slightly damp and smelt of the turf which was kept alongside the garden furniture.

"You should have let me bicycle with you," Avril said good humouredly.

I'd refused to let her come with me into the village on the other bicycle, claiming its brakes were faulty and the hill too steep.

"I'm exhausted," I said. "You wouldn't have enjoyed it."

I glanced round at Eva. Her face was turned toward the sun and her eyes were closed.

"Where are Peake and Malachy?" I asked. They completed the party.

"Gone fishing."

"Do you think they'll catch our supper?"

"I don't know, Avril," I said, for it was she who had asked the question. Then I stopped myself. You must stop sounding like that, I told myself. I didn't need to be a mind reader to understand why Eva had brought Avril along. It's better to go with it than against it, I told myself.

"What I hope," I said, in a conciliatory tone, looking directly across at Avril, "is that they catch a salmon."

"I found some capers in the kitchen," she said, beaming back at me, "that's what we'll cook it with."

She had one leg tucked against her chest and her chin rested on the knee. She was staring at me.

"Here," Eva said. There was a hiss as she levered the top off a bottle of stout.

When I heard Peake and my half-brother returning, I was reading in my bedroom. As in Hampton Wick, my room was in the top of the house where the attic had been. The floor was covered with an unfamiliar matting which gave off a smell like dry grass. There was a small window, a heavy old bed with a duvet, and a copy of Holman Hunt's "Christ with a Lamp" in a buckled frame on the wall.

"Hey Malachy."

Avril came in. On her head she was wearing a garland of daisies which she'd made in the afternoon. Avril was many things but one thing she wasn't was innocent and somehow the chaplet drew attention to that.

"You've got to come down," she said. "Malachy and Peake have something to tell us."

"When I've finished my chapter," I said and held up my book.

"Oh come on," she coaxed, "come now."

"No."

"Then I'll wait."

"How can I read . . ." I started, and she was on the bed and sitting before I finished, ". . . with you sitting there?"

"OK," she said plaintively.

She had agreed to go but she made no move to do so.

"What are you reading?" she asked.

I let out a loud snort of amazement and handed over the book.

"*A Happy Death*," she read carefully, holding her fingers between the pages I was reading. "Is it good?"

"Come on," I said.

I threw the book on to the window ledge. When it landed a small cloud of dust rose into the air. A gust of wind sighed in the copper beech tree behind the house.

In the kitchen, Peake was standing on a chair holding his fishing rod.

"The lake was calm," he said. "The reeds bent before the gentle breeze. Alas, not a bite the live-long afternoon."

"Oh get on with it," said Malachy. He was at the head of the table with the cutlery drawer out and his feet were resting on it.

"I was reeling in, in anticipation of our departure after several fruitless hours," continued Peake, "when suddenly there was a nibble. I stood still. My heart raced. Then – wow!"

He flicked the rod back indicating a strike and with the tip caught the light bulb hanging from the ceiling. It swung about wildly as he continued.

"At last – a bite. But I only had a ten-pound line and I knew I was on to something bigger." He mimed turning the arm of the reel. "I let out the line. Then I came to the end. No more line. So I started moving down the shore, this great fish pulling me on all the time. Then I came to a tree growing right in the middle of my path, right on the water's edge. I couldn't go into the lake – no wellingtons. So . . ."

Peake jumped down from the chair and mimed passing the rod with enormous difficulty around the imaginary tree trunk.

"I had to pass it like this from one hand to the other."

"Get on with it," Malachy interrupted again.

"It was an epic struggle," continued Peake, "of several hours. My wit and ingenuity versus his or her animal cunning; but, in the end, man triumphed."

Malachy took the parcel of newspaper which had been lying on his lap and opened it on the table.

"And here it is," Malachy said, and there, lying on the table with its gun-metal grey speckled back and white belly, was a salmon.

Eva said, "Funny it should have come wrapped in newspaper."

"Actually, we got it gutted," said Malachy, "by a very helpful fishmonger in Letterkenny. He wrapped it too." Malachy looked at his sister and smiled. "We try harder. We think of everything."

I peeled potatoes and put them into the saucepan. When the water boiled I turned down the gas. A yellowish scum trickled over the side and hissed when it hit the flame.

Avril stuffed the salmon, as she had said, with capers. Then she wrapped it in silver paper and put it into the oven to bake.

Peake dismembered and washed the two green lettuces and dried the leaves in a tea towel.

Malachy sat at the bread board cutting a clove of garlic into tiny fine pieces. He collected these up on the blade and scooped them into the jam-jar holding the dressing.

Eva stood over a bowl, dropping olive oil dribble by dribble into egg yolk and whisking the mixture furiously. We all gathered round to watch. The elements began to blend; staring at the bowl, I had the impression the dark yellow of the yolk was draining away; gradually, in front of our eyes, the mayonnaise appeared.

We sat around the table to wait, drinking whiskey. I drank two measures, each time draining the glass with my head back and letting the ice cubes knock against my front teeth.

The fish was taken from the oven and the silver paper peeled back. A pink watery liquid oozed from the slit along its belly. I stared at the large white eye on the side of its head. I must be drunk, I thought. It felt good though.

We lit the candles and started to eat. The pale pink flesh was moist and peeled easily from the bones.

Malachy opened the cookery book which Eva had consulted before making the mayonnaise.

"Do not attempt to make mayonnaise if a thunderstorm is imminent or in progress," he read, "for the ingredients simply will not bind."

"Of if you have your period," Avril added.

A long discussion followed. Peake argued it was nonsense. It was just another way to make women feel insecure about their biology. Eva and Avril demurred. Why couldn't there be a relationship between two events, even if there was no direct link? they argued. What was more, old wisdoms often contained truths which modern science ridiculed only because it couldn't explain them. The conversation drifted away to pyramids and premonitions but returned to the original issue. Quite a fierce row developed. Peake accused Eva and Avril of wanting to be denigrated. They argued back that he was arrogant. He wanted them, Avril and Eva said, only to understand their physiologies as he did. But they wouldn't. They would see them as *they* wanted. There was a good chance, perhaps even a certainty, they concluded, that for four days of the month they couldn't make good mayonnaise.

I took no part in the discussion but sat there, listening, eating and drinking. Once or twice I found myself looking across at Avril and smiling.

Later, still drinking, I sat alone while the others cleared. There was a back scullery where Malachy was washing the dishes and Eva was drying them. I heard Malachy laughing and Eva shouting, 'You monster, you liar . . .'

He ran into the room. There were soap suds on his hands. Eva pursued him, flailing at his back with the wet tea towel.

"You lying toad," Eva called out but she was laughing as well. "I'll never trust you and Peake again."

They faced each other from opposite ends of the table.

"Do you know what?" she said to me. "They didn't catch that bloody salmon. They bought it."

Malachy laughed uproariously. She threw the tea towel at him and he caught it. After he threw it back, he dropped from sight and started to crawl along under the table. I felt him brush past my feet. He came out at the other end and scampered towards Eva. She fended him off with one hand and flicked with the tea towel. Malachy gripped her bare leg just above the knee. She tried to pull her skirt down and push him away. He squeezed.

"No, Malachy," she shouted, laughing and screaming at the same time. "No horse bites." She sat down on the floor.

At the front of the house there was a parlour with large sofas and cushions. I lit a fire in the grate and Eva laid the Scrabble board on the floor. Avril put the tiles into a Quinnsworth plastic bag and we selected seven each.

We had a one litre bottle of Power's whiskey. As we played we all slowly drank from it.

At the start of the game my powers of concentration were low. I couldn't look at the tiles along my rack and see, amongst the confusion, combinations making words. I drank some more and the ability mysteriously appeared. My scores began to rise. I stopped hearing what the others were saying.

Some way into the game I laid my head back against the edge of the sofa and closed my eyes. There was a lovely moment of emptiness. Then, what I'd been avoiding came into the centre of my thoughts. So far I had refused to recognise it and I wanted to go on refusing. I opened my eyes again. Maybe by turning out to the real world I could keep it at bay? It was a hopeless idea because what I wanted to elude was right in front of me.

Avril was sitting on the other side of the board. She had her legs tucked under her and she held her white face between her hands. She must have sensed I was looking at her because she raised her head and smiled at me. It was a big, wide smile which showed her small, whitish teeth.

I closed my eyes again and leant back. Before my inner eye I saw words and letters swirling and then I heard Eva saying, "Avril, you cheat."

I looked across at Avril. She was now sitting on her knees and gesticulating adamantly with her arms.

"I wasn't cheating," she said, but with a grin on her face which said the very opposite.

"I saw you putting a piece in the plastic bag and trying to take another one out," said Eva fiercely.

"I didn't," said Avril. "Do you want to see my pieces?"

"No I don't. Give me the plastic bag."

"No," said Avril, snatching it up and holding it against her chest.

"You've only got six pieces, where's your seventh?" asked Peake triumphantly.

"Probably in the bag," said Malachy. "Hand it over."

"I bet she had the 'Q' and put it back," said Peake, "because both the 'U's are out and she can't use them."

"That's not true," exclaimed Avril.

A long and inconclusive wrangle followed during which large amounts of Power's were drunk and everyone made loud, preposterous claims. Avril maintained her innocence which everyone knew was a lie. Eva, Malachy and Peake appeared outraged but didn't really care and we all knew this.

I drank and wondered why Avril had done it? Was it liquor or bravado? Or both? During the most heated moments of discussion she kept looking at me.

The argument fizzled out and we played on until all the tiles were used. The scores were added. I was amazed to discover I was second.

Eva and her brother and Peake said good night and drifted away to bed, and I found myself alone with Avril. She came and sat beside me on the floor, leaning against the sofa.

I heard her saying, "I wish I had some dope."

"Hasn't Peake got some?" I murmured. My eyes were closed.

I forget what we talked about and the next thing I remember was feeling that she had taken my left hand and hearing her saying, "I bet you're ticklish."

"I'm not."

"Round and round the garden, goes the teddy bear," she began, circling a finger around my palm, "One step, two step," she walked two fingers up my arm, "Tickley under there." With her two fingers she worried at my armpit through my shirt. I laughed and opened my eyes. She put both her hands on my stomach. She tickled in such a way there was a chance her fingers might slip under my belt. The next was inevitable.

I gripped Avril's leg above the knee. She screamed and fell back. It was an obvious over-reaction.

I poked at her stomach through her black singlet top. She

wriggled on the floor shouting, "No", between great laughs.

The rush matting beneath caught her clothing; she was making this happen it seemed to me, and as she squirmed her singlet came out of her trousers and her white midriff was exposed.

She started sliding along the floor. Her cotton trousers, catching now on the matting, started to tug down at the back. At the front of her belly I saw the elastic of her knickers.

I brought my hands down and started to squeeze her just above the hips.

She increased the dragging and her trousers slipped a little further down. Squeezing with one hand, I started to roll them off with the other. She wriggled and squirmed but kept her arms firmly above her head. When I'd got them below her knees she started bicycling with her legs in the air. It could have passed for the actions of someone laughing but the effect was to kick free of them. They landed in a heap on the floor.

Her singlet was almost up to her brassiere and I tickled her on her ribs. She heaved and bumped on the floor. Now her knickers caught on the matting and rolled down until the top of her black pubic hair showed.

I put one hand on her stomach and really puckered the flesh. With the other hand I got hold of the elastic. Her arms stayed resolutely over her head. She screamed uproariously. When I got the knickers to her knees she kicked them away.

She stopped laughing and opened her eyes. I put my hand between her legs. The hair was wet. I brought my face to hers and felt her warm tongue pressing against my teeth.

We went upstairs. She went first and I followed. She carried her clothes. On her bottom I noticed a shiny inoculation mark.

She took off the rest of her clothes and bent forward to pull back the covers on my bed. With the light coming from the hall, I could see the outline of her body. She was plump with heavy breasts and short legs.

I undressed, slid into bed beside her and shivered. Avril put an arm around me and started rubbing my back.

"This should warm you up," she said.

"I don't have anything," I said.

I sensed her head shaking on the pillow beside me.

"That's all right. I slipped in my cap before supper."

I put my mouth against Avril's. Her tongue came forward and started to run along my lips. She rolled on to her back. I put my hand on her thigh and ran it upwards. She opened her legs and drew her knees up. Her sex had turned itself outwards. She closed her legs over my hand and then opened them again and then closed them again and then opened them again. Her mouth opened and I felt her small teeth and her broad, warm tongue.

If this is going to be done, I thought, it's best done whole-heartedly.

Lying like that, moving with her, every thought and concern that I had left me and I started to enjoy myself. For how long this went on, I don't know. Minutes I suppose.

A door banged somewhere — or it sounded like a door banging.

"What's that?" murmured Avril, and she put her tongue against my mouth and sighed.

My state of unselfconsciousness vanished and the worst of all thoughts insinuated itself.

Somewhere in the house was Eva. She knew what I was doing. Or in the morning she would find out.

Just when I had least expected, I had found a bedrock of fidelity in myself that was hard and unyielding.

Avril moaned and I felt my sex shrinking inside her. I went on moving my hips but I was flaccid and fell out of her.

"Put it in," she said, and I felt her trying to reach down.

"I'll come," I lied.

I pressed harder with my finger and she let her legs drop completely open, as far as they could go. It was an action of such trust. I pressed even harder and moved my finger faster. She began making little murmuring sighs. Slowly, these grew louder and more frequent. I pressed against her harder still with my finger. Her arms across my shoulders squeezed me tighter. I changed from rubbing with my finger to rubbing with my thumb. I slid two fingers into her, and her sex around them was warm and wet. She gave a long moan and arched herself upwards. She reached down with a hand and put it on mine. I stopped rubbing. My fingers came out. It was over.

I felt her reaching further down with her hand and trying to find my sex.

"Come on," she whispered.

She found me.

"We'll manage," she said.

She cupped one hand around my testicles. With the finger and thumb of the other she started to rub the glans. I felt my penis growing stiff. In the darkness, Avril alternately murmured encouragement and pressed with her warm tongue against the hard, crinkly inner part of my ear.

"Tell me what you're thinking?" she whispered.

I said, "Nothing," and began pushing out of my thoughts the inhibiting anxiety and putting in its place the vague spectral images of torso and breasts and the rest of the female body which play in the mind during love-making. I began to feel the faintest stirrings of desire. Avril worked faster and eventually my semen trickled out. I felt a few warm droplets landing on my belly and heard a faint slithering sound as it got between her fingers.

She slid down the bed and put her mouth around my sex. She squeezed out the last of the semen and swallowed. It was over.

She came back up and lay beside me on the pillow. We were both quite still. I found myself waiting for the sound of even breathing which would signal Avril was asleep.

Since the morning of the kaftan when I'd asked why she got so blue, Eva and I had both fallen in the estimation each had of the other. We'd worked earnestly and successfully at it. I felt a sense of relief now, as I lay waiting for sleep. One further step in the process had been taken, perhaps the most critical of all. At the same time I felt a sense of dread at what I would say the next morning. I hadn't really changed in the way I felt about her, and I didn't think she had changed either towards me.

I started following the rhythm of Avril's breathing and fell into a deep and dreamless sleep.

*   *   *

The next morning we were first up, Avril started making breakfast while I went outside.

There was a breeze which brought out the goose pimples on my arms and sent the white clouds scurrying overhead. I was carrying turf from the shed in a two-handled basket.

The back door was open and Avril was standing inside by the Aga. She was waiting for the toast to cook under one of the lids. She was wearing a denim skirt and a loose top. It only came three-quarters of the way down and so some of her stomach was exposed.

The kitchen door opened and it was Eva. I put down the turf and pretended to restack the pieces on the top. Inside, I saw Eva going straight over to Avril and poking at the bare flesh.

"You can't go on the ferry like that," Eva said, "showing off all that fat."

Avril said, "What side of the bed did you get out of this morning?"

"The same as I always do." Then she added, "The non-tarts' side."

I came into the kitchen and said, "Good morning," as cheerfully as I could manage.

Eva nodded and muttered something which I didn't catch.

I went to the front room. I replaced the turf we'd burnt the night before and swept the hearth for the second time that morning.

When I returned to the kitchen, Avril had gone. Two burnt pieces of toast lay on the table. Eva was drinking a cup of tea.

"How are you this morning?" I asked.

"I hope you know what you're doing," she said.

I could feel the weight of her prepared lecture behind the words. I was being irresponsible; Avril had deep feelings which I had exploited; and so on.

I took a breath and said, "If I did want to find out, which I don't, I wouldn't ask you," and that was the end of our conversation.

Eva didn't talk to me in the car as we drove to Dublin; or on the ferry to Liverpool; or in the car again during the long drive south towards London. She did, however, manage a few curt sentences with Avril.

We stopped at the Watford Gap Service Station. While Peake and Malachy put oil and petrol into the car, Eva went to buy chocolate. Avril and I were finally alone.

"At least she's being angry," Avril said.

"She's a pain."

"It's better than going to bed and not moving."

Avril found my hand and squeezed.

"I wish you could screw me now," she said.

The following morning, back in Hampton Wick, Eva came to my room, knocked and entered before I had a chance to say, "Yes."

"Hello," I said.

Eva was wearing white shorts and an overlarge tee-shirt knotted at the side.

"I thought we had a plan to have a game of badminton every morning," she said. It was true. We did. I dressed quickly and followed her down to the garden . . .

She never referred to what happened in Donegal and three days later she had Avril round to the house.

The old way Eva and I had of speaking to one another is gone, replaced by something not unpleasant but cordial and formal, full stop.

Diary, Hampton Wick

I found a job in The Lunchbox. This is a place near the station which sells snacks to commuters. It is like a cupboard really, with shelves around the edges where the customers sit on high stools, and a counter across the middle.

The kitchen is at the back. Its walls are grey and the floor is covered with linoleum which is greasy and cracked. There are two sinks and a small barred window. This looks out on to the corner of a builder's yard where bricks are stacked. Every Monday I lay Wharfrin poison behind the refrigerator and the deep freeze. Every night the mice run wild, leaving their tell-tale droppings everywhere.

My job is to heat up the food which we serve in the microwave oven, clear away the dishes and wash them. I am paid £2.00 an hour, cash.

I usually get back from work at about 3.20. The house is always empty. Malachy is out driving for Montgomery's the butcher's; Eva is in the chemist's; Teresa is in the town hall in the accounting department; and John is at the pool rooms or one of his other businesses.

Yesterday I closed the front door behind me and stood quite still. This is what I usually do. I always appreciate the silence after the noise at work.

The hall was filled with greenish light. This came from the trees in front of the house. The mahogany table was beside me. There was a plain white bowl on it in which two camellias floated. The petals were cream coloured but brown along the edges. Their rich scent carried right through the house.

The telephone started to ring and it made me jump. I hurried through to the kitchen. I turned off the telephone-answering machine and picked up the receiver.

"Is Teresa, is Mrs O'Neill there?"

"No I'm afraid she's not, Mrs Gara. She's at work."

"I've tried work. They said try home."

"She'll certainly be back later."

"I want her now."

"She usually gets back some time after six."

There was a sigh followed by a long silence.

After a few moments I began to wonder if Mrs Gara was still there. I couldn't say, "Are you still there?" so I said instead, "Can I take a message?"

"A kutyám . . ." she began in Hungarian, and then correcting herself continued, "My dog is dead."

There was another silence and I heard the unmistakable sound of sobbing.

"Mrs Gara, can I do anything to help?" I asked.

"Yes. Take him away. The porter won't take him until tomorrow and I couldn't stand having him here all night. It's driving me crazy. My heart is broken."

I noticed the smell of the washing-up powder we used at The Lunchbox. It came from the hand with which I was holding the receiver.

I took a note of her address and promised Mrs Gara I would be with her as soon as possible.

I put the phone down and looked at my hands. The fingers were slightly puffy, and the skin around the bottom of the nails was flaking away.

Post-war

By April 1945 the war on the Eastern front was over and the Soviet army was in control of Hungary. One day in the summer, Stephen appeared at the single room where his wife and daughter were living. He had walked from Slovakia where his unit had ended the war.

He had survived for four months because he had had the good sense to bring a sack of typeface with him. Every time he was hungry, he would knock a handful of characters into a lump, polish this until it shone, and then sell it to gullible peasants as silver.

For Teresa he had a present. It was a small gourd pipe, with a sweet, melancholy sound.

The screen went up again. Teresa returned to sleeping on the floor. She was never actually woken by the sound of her parents making love but was often disturbed by it. Whenever she did wake in the night, it was always afterwards, and then what she would hear was the two of them whispering to one another tenderly, and she would smell the coarse cigarettes of black tobacco which they smoked. In the autumn, her mother became pregnant.

By the time the baby was due, it was summer. One mid-morning, Mrs Gara was standing at the window of the room, looking down into the courtyard. Her attention was on an old woman, beating a threadbare carpet on the wooden frame provided for that purpose. Mrs Gara was following the flat-ended cane carpet-beater shuttling back and forth, and the clouds of dust which hung in the air before vanishing like ghosts, when she felt the first contraction.

Teresa was sitting on the stairs with a small boy who was letting her try on his thick, distorting spectacles. When they were in place, the stair banister appeared to expand and to swim in front of Teresa's eyes.

Mrs Gara called her daughter in. They put on their coats, although it was a warm day, and Mrs Gara picked up the bag which she had packed in readiness. Inside there was a nightdress, a toothbrush, a comb which was missing three tines, and newspaper cut into squares ready for the lavatory.

They left word with a neighbour for Stephen when he returned from work, and walked to the tram stop. While they waited Mrs Gara leant against a railing. When the contractions came, she held the handle of the bag very tightly and closed her eyes.

The tram appeared, sparks flying from under its wheels, and screeched to a halt. They climbed aboard and found a seat. With a jolt the tram set off. Mrs Gara let out a little cry. One or two of the other passengers looked at her. She had her hands over her eyes and she didn't notice them.

Teresa looked out of the window. She saw buildings half-collapsed or without roofs, or still covered with soot from when they had been on fire; nests of tangled tram track just thrown to the side of the road; streets with huge shell holes or ditches.

Around these areas of dereliction she also saw there were people busily working: taking down the wrecked buildings and putting up new ones in their place; carting off the tram tracks; filling in the holes and laying cobblestones to make roads.

The hospital was a big, squat, square building with ugly windows. An orderly was assigned to show Mrs Gara and Teresa the way. It was a long, slow painful climb to the fifth floor.

When they arrived, they found the labour ward was a single, enormous room. There were beds along the walls, filled with women in various stages of labour. There was absolutely no privacy. It was also completely full. Teresa knew, if she let herself, she would easily cry.

The orderly led them back outside and brought them to a small, dark stub of corridor, which ran down the side of the ward. He dragged a bed out of a cupboard, which was already made up. This was to be Mrs Gara's. He told her to undress and get in. "Undress here, in the corridor?" she asked. "Where else?" said the orderly, and went off.

Mrs Gara went into the cupboard, and although it had no light, she closed the door. A few odd sounds drifted from inside. Teresa sat down on the bed to wait. The once white hospital walls were now something closer to yellow. There was no window and little light, and she noticed a strong smell: boiled food, disinfectant, pee and blood, all mixed together.

Mrs Gara came out of the cupboard and climbed into the bed. The orderly returned with a towel and a bowl of steaming water. He told Teresa to go into the ward next door and wait until she was called.

Teresa went into the corridor and doubled-back to the labour room. Round the walls, all the moon-like faces of the patients were turned to the corner. The woman there in the bed was crying out in pain and writhing under the covers. Teresa felt terrified, wished to run, but when she made a move to turn, found her legs paralysed with fear.

Time seemed to slow down and the woman's cries grew louder. A nurse swept past Teresa and went over to the woman. Teresa watched with a growing sense of terror as the covers on the bed came back. She had an impression of legs, arms, belly with the dark dimple of the belly button in the middle, and then she saw there was blood everywhere; on the patient's thighs, on the nurse's pinafore, on the wall and even the bars of the iron bedstead.

"Go away," said a voice and Teresa felt herself being propelled towards a door. One of the other patients was out of bed and bending over her.

"It's not good for a little girl here. Go to your mummy . . ."

Teresa glimpsed the samaritan's breasts through the collar of her nightdress, heavy and swollen.

Teresa sped through the door. She sprinted along the corridor and round the corridor. "Mother, mother . . ."

She found herself at the bottom of the iron bedstead. Mrs Gara had her knees up and her sex wide open. The orderly was shaving her rather briskly between the legs. "Out," he said. Mrs Gara's head lay back on the pillows: her face was white and she appeared to be looking into the distance. Teresa heard the terrible tell-tale sound of her pee splattering on to the floorboards.

Teresa went back to the main corridor and cried with her face to the wall. The warm, wet feeling around her middle gradually became cold and uncomfortable.

As the afternoon wore on, the contractions grew worse. Mrs Gara, who had no-one with her, sent Teresa to find someone.

Teresa ran out into the corridor and stopped a man. He didn't understand what she was saying. Nor did the second person. Then a nurse asked her what she was doing and Teresa led her to her mother.

The nurse took Mrs Gara's pulse and felt her stomach and then left, promising to return.

The contractions grew still worse. Mrs Gara started screaming. She told Teresa to find help. Her daughter ran to the corridor. She had forgotten now about the moist, sticky feeling around her middle.

She opened doors along the corridor but found they only led to rooms filled with beds of sick people and no-one who could help her. On the stairs Teresa found a man in a white coat but he wouldn't come. Two men in coats pushing a trolley finally agreed to follow her. They took Mrs Gara's pulse again and left, promising to return.

A few minutes later, when they had not returned, and when the pains became still worse, Teresa was sent off again. She found someone: they came: they left. This went on all afternoon.

At half-past six the baby finally came, blue-faced with the cord around his neck. The nurse who had finally appeared took the corpse straight away, and then Stephen came and took Teresa back to their room.

Mrs Gara came home from the hospital a couple of days later. She sewed little black mourning squares onto the collar of her coat. She hardly spoke and often, when Teresa came in from playing on the landing or in the courtyard, she would find her mother crying.

One afternoon, only a few weeks later, Teresa accidentally dropped the only plate the family possessed. It broke in half. Mrs

Gara, who was peeling a potato by the sink, threw down the knife she was holding and the potato, and started shouting. A few moments later she stripped her daughter and began to beat her on the body.

Teresa's howls were heard in the courtyard. One neighbour came to the door to see if anything was the matter and was told to go away. When Stephen came home from work that evening, he found his daughter hiding under the bed. Her hair was matted and wet with tears, and her cheeks were stained with them. Mrs Gara was in the chair by the window crying quietly. On the floor the two halves of the plate still lay where they had fallen, side by side.

Diary, Hampton Wick

Mrs Gara was clearly waiting for me because after I had pressed her bell she shouted from inside,

"Is that you?"

"Yes."

The door swung back and I saw her pale face in the dark hallway. Around her eyes the skin was puffy and reminded me of an uncooked sausage. Her cheeks were powdered and there was fresh lipstick around her mouth. I took this as a sure sign she had been crying. I suddenly felt the very last thing I'd ever expected to feel for Mrs Gara – a twinge of sympathy.

"Come in."

With a sweep of her little puffy arm she motioned me forward.

The door closed behind. I had forgotten the dog's name and as I was wondering how to get around this she said,

"Dick's in here"

I followed her to the living room. There was a faint fishy smell.

"There."

He was on the armchair under the window, stretched out as if he were asleep.

"I was very sorry," I said and then correcting myself I continued, "I am very sorry."

"He was my best friend."

Mrs Gara pulled a tissue from her pocket and wiped her nose.

"He had been poorly for the last few days. I gave him some boiled chicken at lunchtime but he wouldn't eat it and he always eats his chicken. He came in here and got onto the chair. Normally I wouldn't let him sleep there. I am very strict about that. Normally he has to sleep in his bag." She waved at the paper bag under the table. "But this once I decided to let him. He was not well. Then I saw he was not breathing. I felt him and he was cold."

Mrs Gara's eyes filled with tears.

I stood awkwardly. I could hear the aquarium bubbling. I could hear sniffling. I could hear traffic in the distance. As I stood there I could feel myself starting to get anxious that I was going to have to touch the corpse.

"Where is Teresa?" said Mrs Gara quietly.

The dead dog's fur had been trimmed and the skin below showed through. One of the ears had flapped back over the crown of the head so that the pink inside with its ridges and creases showed. The legs were so thin they looked as if they might snap.

"She is never there when I need her," Mrs Gara continued. "I have to rely on a stranger."

One didn't have to know Mrs Gara very well to sense she was about to start a speech against her daughter on which she'd been brooding for hours. I didn't want to hear.

"Have you got a box?" I asked curtly.

"Of course I have a box. I had the caretaker bring me one. It's one of the few useful things he's ever done for me."

It was in the kitchen on the table.

"It looks too small."

"You haven't tried it yet."

I carried the box into the living room and tried it for size on Dick. His head stuck out beyond one edge and his hindquarters beyond the other.

"Too bloody small," I said quietly to myself.

I returned to the kitchen. Mrs Gara was looking out the window.

"Rubbish bags?" I asked.

She opened a drawer and drew out a packet of swing-bin liners. They were white, vaguely transparent and, as I knew from experience, they were flimsy.

"No black ones?"

"What do you want? These are what you asked for?"

"Any gloves?"

"Are you going to do this for me or what?"

"Sure I am. I simply asked if you had any gloves?"

"No, I haven't. I've had a lifetime of housework without them and I've never seen the need for them."

I carried the plastic bags next door and peered at Dick. Under the eyes there were two crescent-shaped patches. They had always been wet when Dick had been alive and they were still wet. There was the faint smell which dogs give off after they have been in the rain. It was then I noticed the protrusion shaped like a flame between the back legs, the exact colour of a raspberry. The dog had died with an erection.

My mother's words now came back to me: "Nothing's ever as bad as it seems but the longer you think about it, the worse it'll be." When as children she had said this, my sisters and I had always groaned and said it was trite. At the same time I knew it was true.

"I'm boiling the kettle," Mrs Gara shouted through the wall. "You want a cup of coffee?"

I took the bag and cracked it in the air a couple of times until it filled with air. I dragged over a chair and stretched it open over the back.

I got hold of Dick by the neck. He didn't feel cold as I had expected. I lifted him up. The corpse seemed unusually light. The legs stuck straight out from the body.

Let this please be quick and simple I thought.

I held the bin liner with one hand and, holding the dog with the other, attempted to get its rear end in. The problem was the carcass was stiff whilst the bag had no shape whatsoever. It obstructed my manoeuvres by sticking to the fur or itself. Finally, I tried just pulling the mouth of the bag to me and letting the dog go. By a happy fluke I hoped it would just drop through to the bottom. I was not to be rewarded. Instead of disappearing, Dick slid sideways and tumbled on to the floor.

"Sugar," Mrs Gara shouted.

"No."

"It's on the table."

I picked Dick up and rammed him into the bag. He started to

slide down. Great, I thought. Then I saw the sharp nails of his front paws had cut through the plastic and were sticking out. I could remember having had just this problem with a fir tree one Christmas.

I got another bag and put the first one inside it. The paws cut through that bag as well.

Then I had a brilliant idea. I got the brown paper bag in which Dick had slept. I dropped it over his paws and crushed it around them. Then I carefully dropped the two plastic bags with the body inside into a third. This time, no tear. For safety I put everything into a fourth sack and I tied the top.

I went out to the kitchen. My coffee was on the table. I picked it up.

"Sit," said Mrs Gara.

"I've been sitting all day," I lied. "I'd rather stand."

"Where will you put him?"

"In the garden I think."

I wanted to finish the coffee and get out.

"Will you see Teresa?"

"Yes."

"She's never around when I need her."

Should I answer her back, I wondered?

There doesn't seem to be any point, came the answer. Nothing you can say will make any difference.

Still, she shouldn't be allowed to get away with it, I replied, and if I don't say something I'll only loathe myself for it later.

Not worth it.

As I saw my two choices ahead of me, like forked paths in a wood, another of my mother's sayings came to me. It is funny how I rely on her platitudes in times of difficulty:

"Always treat others as you would like to be treated yourself." As I would want myself to be defended from an unfair attack so, I decided, I should do the same here. My virtue was motivated by self-love.

"It wasn't Teresa's fault she was at work. If she'd been at home, I'm certain she'd have come over and sorted everything out."

Mrs Gara looked at me with her small dark eyes.

"I lay sixteen hours in labour in a Budapest hospital," she

began, spitting out the words with extraordinary vehemence and speaking with uncustomary speed. "Could she find me the doctor? No. When you need her, Teresa is never there."

So that's what she's been brooding on, I thought. This came from the part of my mind which looks down from a height and appraises coldly.

It was from another part that I spoke.

"You cannot blame Teresa for being at work today."

"After my ordeal," said Mrs Gara ferociously, at the same time slicing the air to signal the end of something, "no more children. A man can't understand of course."

My thighs were trembling. I was certain my voice was going to waver when I next opened my mouth. I was angry.

"That has nothing to do with it."

"Don't answer me back, young man."

"I'm twenty-five. I'm not answering back. I'm attempting to speak to you."

"I don't care how old you are."

"I can't allow you to run Teresa down unfairly."

"She's my daughter. You are nothing."

I've always thought the argument – "You're not family, so stay out of it" – one of the lowest. I decided not to say any more and instead to communicate my feelings by staring at her as I drank my coffee. Mrs Gara stared back. It was like one of the ridiculous contests of will I used to have at school.

The cup was dry. "Thanks," I said and left the kitchen. Was she going to say "Thank you" and "Goodbye" I wondered? I opened the front door and stood for an instant waiting. Nothing.

I picked up the plastic bags, stepped out and closed the door behind.

On the train to Waterloo, the paper bag which I had put over the paws came away. The nails tore a hole in the plastic and Dick's two front legs dropped out.

Arriving at Waterloo, where I had to change trains, I decided it was pointless to try to hide what I was carrying. I had a perfectly good explanation I told myself, and I had nothing to feel guilty about.

I stepped down on to the platform and swung the load on to

my shoulder as if it were the most natural action in the world. The two woolly drumstick legs were sticking out but no-one appeared to notice as I walked towards the barrier, and certainly no-one paid any attention for the rest of the journey. If it was done naturally, I decided, it would probably be possible to carry a corpse through London, without being challenged by anyone.

I arrived at Hampton Wick after the rush hour. Not many got out of the train with me but on the other platform revellers were already gathering, waiting to take the 'up' to London and their night out. Several of them carried mackintoshes. The warmish summer evenings were already giving way to something colder.

I got back to the O'Neills' house and put my key into the lock. I heard the sound of rapidly approaching footfalls. The door was opened before I could turn the key and there was Teresa. Her face was drawn and she looked unhappy. I could guess why.

"I am sorry," she said. "I have just been speaking to my mother. You've been put to such trouble."

She lifted her hands as if she were to offer to take the plastic sacks from me, then dropped them again and said nothing.

"It was probably just as well he went instead of you," said Malachy. He was sitting on the bottom step of the stairs with the telephone on his knees.

We dug a hole together, he and I, in the garden, in the grey earth near where the cuttings mouldered, dropped Dick in and covered him over. We expended a good deal of energy levelling the bump with the flat of our spades until there was no sign of the grave.

We were tired. We went and sat in the canvas chairs under the apple trees and each lit a cigarette.

"How did Mrs Gara come to this country?" I asked.

Malachy chortled.

"She came for Christmas, I don't remember exactly when, five, six, seven years ago," he began. "She said she didn't want to go back to the Communists in Hungary. You'll have gathered she doesn't like them very much. She said, 'I want to stay.' Her husband was dead and she was a pensioner by this stage. Mum and Dad 'ummed' and 'aaahhed'. Wouldn't you? Because it was Christmas and that, we had a fire going in the front room, and one evening she fetched her passport and threw it on. 'Now I'm staying,' she said. Of course it wasn't as simple as that. She had to go back to Hungary and apply from there – the immigration laws in this country being such an unbelievable fucking nightmare – which meant getting her a new passport. Then she came. Really, Mum was steam-rollered into it."

At supper Teresa said nothing. She also ate nothing. Afterwards she went straight away to bed. Ten minutes later she called her daughter.

When Eva returned to the kitchen – her mother had asked for a cup of camomile tea – I saw the expression on Eva's face I had seen there before. But now relations were different. I didn't ask or console or probe. I remained silent as she stood waiting for the kettle to boil.

John went to his workshop in the garage. The sound of hammering and sawing drifted through the walls. The familiar atmosphere of depression descended.

Teresa

At the age of thirteen Teresa had become a good-looking girl, with dark blonde hair and wide blue eyes. Like her mother and her grandmother and her great-grandmother before her, she was small and her slim legs were slightly bandy.

She owned two dresses and two pairs of woollen stockings. She went to school in a black skirt and a blouse which she wore with her single cardigan. She owned one pair of shoes and when they were at the cobbler's, she would stay at home or borrow from her mother. She wore small sleepers in her ears. The day before her eleventh birthday her mother had numbed her lobes with lumps of ice provided by the fishmonger, and then pushed a needle through to make the holes, using a cork for a thimble.

It was March. On the insides of the window panes there were little tongues of green mould where the rain seeped through, and over that a thin veil of ice.

There was a knock. Her mother opened the door. Teresa looked up from her biology exercise book where she was drawing a picture of a stamen.

It was Mary, wife of Sándor, neighbours and close friends of the Garas. Teresa sensed an unusual quiet in the building and outside in the courtyard.

Mary came in. There was an extraordinary look on her face. Hilarity was wrestling there with solemnity. Mrs Gara shut the door. "Comrade Stalin," Mary hissed, "is dead."

Stephen did not come home that evening but stayed in the city at his place of work. This was the *Szabad Nép* building, which not only housed the party newspaper of the same name, but a variety of other state publications besides. Stephen did not have a top status job – in the building this would have been a full-time position on *Szabad Nép* – but a job that was one step down. He was a shift worker, moved from concern to concern as the demand for printers required. Despite not being top-notch it was, nonetheless, pretty well paid; it required party membership; and Stephen had long since learnt how to keep his mouth shut. What kept him busy this evening, and well into the early hours beyond, was the *Szabad Nép* special edition on the life and times of the great father, as they called Stalin. It appeared with a black border around each page.

The following morning, Teresa went to catch her tram.

The street was lined with black flags which hung motionless in the cold air. Pedestrians moved carefully below them on the frost-covered pavements, hoar breath curling from their mouths. The atmosphere was subdued and sombre. Teresa was still a girl but she was already wise enough to know exactly what she had to do. She was humble and silent and looked only at the ground, as if she was in a reverie of grief.

The tram appeared in the distance and drew up at the stop. For a moment it had seemed embarrassingly loud, like someone talking in a church or a library.

She climbed on and went and stood by one of the doors. The tram pulled off. Outside the window, one street after another slid by. There were black flags hanging from every lamp post and every building. The whole city was adorned with black flags it seemed. When she arrived at school, she found the portrait of Stalin in the entrance hallway was already decorated with a huge black bow of crepe. Although her mother and father weren't crying at home, she knew it was expected. So she squeezed her eyes tight until she was crying and the tears were rolling down her cheeks.

The day before the funeral, the local secretary of the party's youth organisation, KISZ, came to the school and paid a visit to Teresa's class.

He gave a small talk. The funeral would be a sad and painful occasion but he knew he could rely on the children to distinguish themselves. He explained everyone would assemble in the school yard, cross by Saint Margaret's bridge over the Danube into Pest, and make their way to the city park where the school would lay a wreath.

Then he took two pupils – Teresa was one – to the store room. All the paraphernalia used for mass meetings was here: flags, portraits and banners. Also rolls of the crinkly red paper which went behind the busts of luminaries. Some of the banners were unfurled. She read "Long Live Mátyás Rákosi: Wise Leader of the Hungarian Working People" and then, "In unbreakable friendship with the Soviet Union we March to Socialism".

Teresa was given the task of mending a Soviet flag. It had a tear across the middle. An hour later the KISZ secretary came to ask her how it was going and took the opportunity to squeeze her knee.

The next day she assembled with the other pupils and marched. When they reached Stalin's statue, she found the whole surrounding area jammed with people. No mass event had been like this and she had been to two or three. For some reason, instead of the mourners entering on one side and leaving on the other, they streamed in from all sides, filling the area beyond what it could hold.

All around her, Teresa saw heads and felt bodies pressing against her. In the distance was the statue of the moustachioed Soviet leader. He stood on pink steps, wearing a pair of enormous, knee-high boots. She dropped her beret but there was no possibility of bending down to pick it up. Waves of energy passed through the crowd in different directions, moving her one way and then the other. She wondered if it was like being in the sea? She had only read about the ocean and had no way of knowing.

Teresa got home some hours later. She found her mother and father waiting in their room. Stephen and his wife had been in the square too, with colleagues from their work places. When they had got home and not found Teresa there, they had started to worry. Now they embraced her.

In the evening, Teresa made up her bed. She slept on a divan now, which doubled up as a sofa in the day. Her parents slept on the iron bedstead they had always had behind the screen.

She washed from a bowl at the sink and climbed under the duvet. When she closed her eyes, she could feel the crowd pushing just like they had, and she felt the sensation of being carried in one direction and then the other. In recollection it was a strange, not unpleasant feeling.

At the same time, in her mind's eye, she saw what she had seen. Heads: women's heads with coiled hair or loose hair or long hair tied various ways; men's heads with hair black or fair, long and ragged or shaved so closely the white of the scalp showed through the bristles. Above the heads and far away was the statue of Stalin, standing on pink steps with the inscription beneath: *A Nagy Sztálinnak a hálás Magyar Nép*, To the great Stalin from the grateful Hungarian people.

She forgot about the day, the statue and the terrible crush until the spring, when she was at another mass gathering with heads all around her and a figure in the distance. This was Parliament square and far away on the balcony of the Parliament building was the squat figure of Mátyás Rákósi with his bald head.

Teresa paid no attention to what he was saying. This was relayed to the crowd through speakers which were dotted around. She stared at those who were nearest: a young girl with big gold earrings and hair the colour of straw; two workmen in boiler suits which shone with grease; a woman in peasant costume who was sucking the end of her plait and then stroking her face with it.

She felt Stephen beside her touching her arm with the point of his elbow. Looking forward and up, she saw the Prime Minister and Party Secretary gesticulating with his arms. Then she caught something about an economic plan so daring the enemy had contemptuously called it a Communist bluff.

Teresa heard her father laughing at this remark. The girl with the straw-coloured hair, the two workmen, and the peasant woman all looked around at him.

Her father smiled at them and clapped as if applauding what was being said. There was an instant of stillness as everyone stared, which seemed to Teresa to drag on and on. All around meanwhile, the crowd shuffled as they listened to the Party First Secretary. Then the girl with the straw-coloured hair applauded along with Stephen. Everyone's eyes returned to the front and the incident was forgotten. Teresa started looking around herself again.

In the evening the family sat down at the oilcloth-covered

table to supper. There were a few pieces of wafer-thin salami and dry bread. Her father drank wine. After two or three glasses he said, "How's this for a joke? Someone from the Party was sent to a village incognito. His job was to find out what the villagers thought about our great leader, Rákosi. He fell into conversation with the barman in a local inn, and over a glass of wine tried to sound the man out. The barman said, 'Not here, come outside.' In the yard he said, 'I don't like it here, let's go a little bit further.' In the street the barman said, 'Let's go on.' Finally, they found themselves in the middle of a field with not a house in sight, and the barman leaned over and said, 'I have to confess, I rather like him.'"

For some reason Teresa remembered the very first moment that winter when she had seen the streets lined with black flags, and how everyone had appeared to be creeping about the city with long and serious expressions. There was an atmosphere about that moment which seemed to forbid what she feared she was about to succumb to.

She saw her mother laughing and taking a glass of wine; her father smiling. He poked her in the ribs. She started laughing with them. She laughed until the muscles of her stomach ached.

A month later, Mrs Gara bought a length of material to make her daughter a summer dress. It had a pattern of big yellow sunflowers on it. The buttons for the back were more difficult. There were none which were suitable in the People's stores and none to be found on the black market. Eventually, in a cobbler's, the only shop left in a parade (all the others had been closed down in the drive against private enterprise), Mrs Gara was able to buy four white buttons which the cobbler's wife turned out herself on a little machine hidden in a cupboard.

It was July by the time the dress was finished and the buttons were on. It had short sleeves, a round collar and ended just below the knee. It had no waist but a line instead under the bust. Teresa put it on for the first time, one afternoon just after she had come home from school.

Later, her father offered to take her for a walk. She would wear the dress of course.

They went down the dark stone stairs, through the courtyard

under washing lines which criss-crossed like telephone wires, and out into the street.

It was a summer's evening. The lamps above the middle of the road threw down beams of pale, white light. There were people about, many of them talking loudly and excitedly.

They reached the corner. The family who lived in the basement under a private photographic shop which had been closed down had carried their radio out on to the pavement. The lights behind the tuning dial glowed in the twilight.

A small crowd had gathered. They were all men from the neighbourhood and Teresa recognised all of them in their short sleeved shirts and berets. A piece of music by Zoltán Kodaly was playing to which no-one was paying any attention. They were all too busy talking animatedly.

Stephen started questioning Sándor, their neighbour and the husband of Mary. Rákosi was gone it appeared. The new Prime Minister was Imre Nagy. The Five Year Plan, the one so daring the capitalists had dubbed it a Communist bluff, was out. Its targets were unrealisable. In its place was the more modest New Government Programme. Teresa didn't quite understand the details but she could feel in her belly it was important.

Stephen was so excited he opened a bottle of spirits when he got back to the room. Teresa fell asleep to the sound of her parents talking and drinking together behind the screen.

In the months which followed the changes started. Street after street in Budapest, away from the main thoroughfares, had been dismal places, of shops with rusty shutters down and faded trade names still visible, closed by the Party's drive against private enterprise. As Teresa noticed wherever she went, they now began to open again; not all but a good many of them.

On Saturdays, when her mother would take her sometimes over the river into Pest, they would stop and look at the new model shops in Rákosi street. For the first time, there were goods properly on display in the windows: lengths of cloth, eggs and cheese, bottles of wine.

In the autumn ten thousand goods were reduced in price. Teresa was impressed though, as Stephen said, each different size of saucepan, each different coloured sweet, each different length of needle was counted as a separate item in order to reach the magical figure of ten thousand.

Then in the early weeks of 1955, Imre Nagy disappeared. It was announced he was ill. That he had coronary thrombosis.

In March, *Szabed Nép* published details of a Party resolution. The policies of the New Government Programme were right-wing, anti-party, anti-Marxist. Nagy was the first propagator. Rákosi was back.

Stephen brought the early edition home from work. He sat down at the oilcloth-covered table and threw it across to his wife. He fetched out his party card, spat on it, and threw it on the floor. Mária told him not to be such a fool. She didn't like it any more than he did, but it was their meal ticket, and that was all that counted. The card lay there for a while longer, and then Stephen retrieved it and wiped the phlegm away with a piece of coarse newspaper, torn from the early edition.

Teresa was sitting on the divan with her schoolbooks. She loathed the card. Secretly, she wished her father had left it. She didn't share her mother's practical outlook. She was not old enough to understand compromise. Then she saw her father's eyes were filled with tears. "I feel hopeless," he said quietly. It was the first time Teresa could ever remember seeing him like this.

Diary, Hampton Wick

The first signs of autumn have begun to show. In the mornings it is cold when I step into the O'Neills' garden at seven or half-past for the customary game of badminton. Through the soles of my shoes I sense the ground below is losing its heat, and a little more every day, and as I run about the drops of dew which have started to appear on the grass get kicked up and splatter my legs. Once or twice, walking to work, I have just perceived a faint mist rising and hanging in the lower branches of the trees. In the evenings, where before I have happily gone out in just a shirt, I now have to remember to take a jersey. Of course, the days continue warm and summery, which accentuates the poignancy of the change in seasons. It seems unfair the two should lie side by side; warmth by day and cold by night.

My time to leave is approaching. On Saturday afternoon, I went to Bentalls with Malachy and bought Teresa a set of china as a present. I chose Warmstry which was plain white. It cost me a good deal of money but I thought, What the hell. We carried them back, unpacked the pieces from boxes filled with straw, and washed them. Malachy put the chain on the front door, so that if his mother had come back, we would have time to hide everything.

I made my arrangements with The Lunchbox. I will work for the remaining three weeks, right up to my last Friday. I will pack on Saturday. On Sunday I will go.

I made enquiries about a mini-cab to Heathrow. Teresa heard me speaking to the company on the telephone. After I had finished she said, "We wouldn't dream of you going to the airport by yourself."

As I stood there I saw the whole scene ... Putting my baggage into the boot and then all of us cramming into the Sierra. John touching the knobbly St Christopher's medal stuck to the dashboard, as he always does before any journey. The air freshener, jingling under the rear-view mirror, and filling the car with the synthetic smell of pine. The quiet streets, deserted because it will be a Sunday morning, gliding by beyond the windows. Heathrow; late holiday makers in summer clothes, and the Asian cleaners, padding through the crowds, women with long sad faces. The announcement board and my flight at the top of the list with the message *Now Boarding*. Saying goodbye to each of the family in turn, seeming cheerful but knowing that as soon as I am in the lounge and alone, surrounded by the Duty Free shops with their gaudy displays, I will feel desolate ... I would rather avoid it all. I want to shake hands at their front door and leave alone, but Teresa was adamant. So I agreed.

Following this, I have since found myself at night, before I get into bed, unable to resist the urge to get my ticket out. I stare at my name written on it, and the date and the time beside it. I am horrified and fascinated by it, like a rabbit caught in the headlamps of a car. I want to put off the moment of my leaving for ever, and at the same time I can't wait for it to come quickly enough. The thought of having to live each second until the time to go actually comes is unbearable and yet I wouldn't give up a single second of it either. I want to stay for ever but I know I am also longing to go. I want the O'Neills to become my family but I long to be back with my own. I secretly wish for some cataclysmic event which will prevent me starting college, and yet I know that if this happened I would be devastated, and that when I do start my course, I will be delighted that I have.

After a while, holding in my mind these irreconcilables exhausts me. I put away my ticket and fall asleep. In the mornings I find it hard to get up, and I notice that my spirits then tend to be morose.

To cheer myself up (that is what I think I am doing), I have started seeing Avril. She comes by work in the afternoon and I bring her home. For the few minutes we are in bed, everything is forgotten. Afterwards, we pull our clothes on hurriedly, terrified now that we might be caught, and say goodbye until the following afternoon.

With each day that passes, I can sense Avril growing more attached. One afternoon, I even heard myself promising that she could come to stay with me in New Jersey for Christmas. When, today, she gave me a present, a new leather strap for my wristwatch and asked "Love me?" I said, "Yes." I felt bad as soon as I had spoken but I left it.

I threaded my watch on to the strap (my old one had been destroyed working at The Lunchbox) and walked her to the end of the street.

"I'll see you tomorrow," she said.

I said, "No", steeling myself for a look of disappointment.

Then she said, "Oh yes, it's Eva's birthday tomorrow. You and the family are going off, aren't you?"

I'd forgotten she would have known. She was Eva's friend.

"Anyway," she continued, "I'll see you in the evening. I'm coming over for the party. I hope you have a nice time."

She put her hands on my shoulders and kissed me on the lips.

"You are a lucky so and so. I'd love to go on one of those flights," she said.

In the evening Malachy and I took Eva out for a pre-birthday drink. She insisted on sitting between us, wedged in a corner like a frightened animal, drank steadily and said nothing. We tried asking her a few questions but in answer to each she either shrugged or mumbled, "I don't want to talk about that." Malachy and I began to talk to one another across the table and she stayed in her corner and said nothing.

Two or three drinks later, Malachy said to his sister, "We might as well have left you at home." "Don't tell me I don't contribute," she replied. "I'll scream if I hear Teresa or you or Dad or anyone say that one more time." Then Malachy said, "Sometimes you can be a pain in the bum," to which she had replied, "My privilege," and got up and went to the bar to buy another round of drinks. We were meant to be paying for everything but we didn't stop her.

When she came back with the drinks and sat down, I said, "Are you looking forward to tomorrow? Are you excited?"

"No," she said.

Her face was the way it always was. Her eyes were still blue. Her eyebrows still arched. Her cheek bones were the same. Even her lips were covered with the lipstick she always wore. But the expression was of someone in misery.

"I'm not."

"Why?" her brother asked.

She shrugged her shoulders. "I don't know."

Her answer was so direct I believed at once she didn't know, and that with anything else we might have offered, her answer would have been the same. Nothing would have interested her.

"I'm in a large, black lagoon of treacle," she said, "and I'm disgusted with myself for being in it." Then she added, "I want to go."

We brought her home. She wouldn't talk to us. She went straight to bed. I wrapped her present. I got my ticket out of the drawer and stared at it. I fell asleep.

The next day was Friday. I woke up early. I felt the wave of anxiety, which comes automatically every time I wake up and think I have to get out of bed and go to work, until I remembered. I had the day off work. Through the wall I heard the door of Malachy's cupboard creaking as it was opened. He was up.

"Hello," I called.

A few moments later, my bedroom door opened and there he was.

"Morning," he said.

Dangling on the end of each forefinger was a wide hoop earring made of gold.

"Do you think she'll like them?"

"Why wouldn't she?"

"Moody last night wasn't she?" He glanced at the long slim package which was my present to Eva. It was lying on the window ledge.

"I don't know if I would have said she was moody."

"You mean she's in pain," he replied, "like everyone else in the family and it goes back generations." His tone was mocking.

"Is it something to do with what's-his-name? Peake."

"He's arranged this morning's jaunt, so it can't be."

He picked up my present to Eva by the gold twine around it, tested its weight and put it down again.

"I'll tell you what it is. When I was about nine and Eva was about seven, Mum took us for a walk to Richmond Park. I've never forgotten this. We went into the Isabella plantation, which is a formal garden. It was a Sunday. Lots of families with their children. By the side of the path some toadstools had sprung up. They were enormous and beautiful. Teresa started this long reminiscence about her grandfather's village and gathering mushrooms on the Hungarian plains in the early morning, et cetera, when this little boy, this little brat, ran up and started kicking these beautiful toadstools, and kicked them and kicked them and kicked them, scattering pieces everywhere, and went on until he had completely destroyed them. His parents came up and took him away. Eva started to cry. When Mum asked her what was the matter, she was inconsolable. All we could get out of her was that the toadstools were so beautiful and she couldn't stand seeing them destroyed."

He looked out of the window.

"She's too sensitive which is obvious and not very helpful. It seems to be a condition in the family. They've all got it going back generations. I, of course, have been let off scot-free for some reason, and the only other person who's had that privilege is Mrs Gara, whatever that means."

He laughed gently and shook his head.

1956

It was October 23rd. A Tuesday. Teresa was sixteen. When she came out of school she buttoned her coat up to the collar. It was cold and in the air there was a sense of what the coming winter would be like.

When she got home she lit the stove and put on the pan of coffee left over from breakfast. On the surface of the coffee there was a film. It seemed to have many colours in it like petrol on the river.

When the coffee was hot, she put it in a mug – the only mug they had – and sat down on the chair by the window.

In the courtyard below there were a few children in coats and carrying satchels, making their way home from school. Two workmen in boots with wooden soles, which didn't bend and so forced them to walk in a peculiar way, carried a length of heavy pipe in from the street. She noticed a young man lolling against a wall and smoking a cigarette. His name was Zoltán. He was a black marketeer and sometimes Stephen bought white nylon shirts from him.

Teresa began studying her periodic table. She was going to be tested on it the following morning. It started to grow dark. She went to turn on the electric light and wondered where her mother was? She was usually home by this time.

When, half-an-hour later, Mrs Gara had still not returned, Teresa began to worry. It was an irritating, gnawing sensation. She found she couldn't concentrate on her work.

She went to the room next door but Mary, the woman who lived there, had no idea where her mother might be. Mary herself was anxious. Sándor, a labourer, had been due back from work for over an hour.

Perhaps something had happened in the city? she suggested. An accident which had closed a bridge and this had led to chaos on the others? Or a seizure in the tram system?

Teresa took her coat from her room, went down to the courtyard, through the archway and into the street.

It was quite dark by now. The lamps slung across the middle of the road were casting their pools of pale light. Workmen in overalls and women with string bags holding a turnip or a small piece of meat wrapped in paper or a single onion were hurrying home.

She walked to the corner. Five streets intersected here and this was where the tram stop was. She watched the trams coming along the rails from the centre of the city and the passengers climbing down. Twice she was certain she saw her mother. With her arms rising for an embrace and the words of greeting on the tip of her tongue, she started to move towards the person, only to discover a fraction of a second later it was not who she thought. It was just a woman wearing a blue gabardine coat and a beret, like her mother, with the same small frame and bandy legs.

As it grew later, the number of passengers alighting from the trams grew smaller. The rush of people to get home from work was over. At the same time, there was an increase in the numbers coming to wait at the stop. Mostly those coming were young men and their girls. They talked loudly and were boisterous with one another, in a way which seemed to Teresa to be false. Now and again, in the cold evening air, there was the smell of scent.

From an elderly gentleman she found out what the time was. Stephen these days was working on the early shift, and she calculated her father would be home in an hour to two hours' time. She decided that rather than go to the police station to ask about her mother, she would wait for him to return.

She went home and as she was opening the door of the room, Mary, who had heard her, came out on to the landing. She was carrying her baby son George. Something was going on in the city, Mary said. She had heard rumours from other neighbours. There had been a large demonstration by students from Eötvös Lóránd university. This was where Teresa's mother worked. Perhaps she had been involved? Mary's husband Sándor was not back yet. She invited Teresa to share some bread covered with lard and sprinkled with paprika. All the time she was eating, Teresa couldn't stop wondering what was going on in the city. Perhaps there were soldiers out on the streets. After the weeks of disturbances and agitations, anything was possible yet it didn't bear thinking about.

Stephen always came home, not by tram but on the lorry which, having delivered paper and other goods to his workplace in the early evening, returned to its depot passing close to Stephen's district. As soon as she had finished bolting her food, Teresa pulled on her coat and left, promising to return if she had any news.

She walked smartly towards the main street where the lorry dropped her father off, breaking into a run for the last hundred yards.

She arrived well before the time the lorry was due and there was no sign of Stephen of course. Only a group of young men, high-spirited and boisterous. They had a look of purposefulness about them, as they surged along the pavement towards Teresa.

"There's a big fight," shouted the first, jerking his thumb back in the direction of the centre of Budapest.

Teresa stepped directly in front of their path.

"What?"

"There's a big fight. We're going to throw the government out."

The young men hurried past like water around a boulder.

"We're going to get the people out of the factories." The speaker waved towards the two smoking chimney stacks further down the road. "Come on. Come with us. We're going to get everybody out."

They were past and speeding away down the street. Teresa took a couple of steps after them, stopped, turned, and looked in the direction from which they had come. She wanted to run after them. She wanted to run forward into the city to see what was happening. A big fight? she thought. What kind of a fight? Everyone coming out? On what? On strike? No strikes allowed. Her thoughts came rapidly and at the very back of them there was one big thought, the government really was going, but it was so extraordinary she didn't let herself dare think it. Run. Go on, her thoughts continued. Go and see. No, wait. Wait for your father. Wait for your mother. What will they do if they return to the room and find you missing? That settled it. She would go home. She would wait. She felt better. She had made a decision.

She went home. Mary had left her room, taking the baby with her, so Teresa had no-one to tell what she had seen. She washed herself with cold water at the sink and got into bed. From outside the window there immediately came a multitude of noises: feet on cobblestones; voices calling; lorries rumbling. Something monumental was happening. She strained her ears, listening for the sound of footsteps on the stairs; all night they sounded but there were none which came to her door. Half a dozen times she turned on the light, looked at her pile of clothes and considered getting dressed and going in to the centre of the city to find her mother and father. Hoping to find two people amidst thousands? her thoughts always ran when she did this, mocking her intentions. Invariably she turned the light off and got back into bed.

At some point in the night, anxious but also exhausted, Teresa fell asleep. She was woken when her mother came home in the early hours of the morning.

Mrs Gara smelt of smoke. She was in a state of excitement. She told Teresa what had happened in a great rush. The university students had marched. The whole city had come out to join them. They had ended up in front of the Parliament building. Imre Nagy had appeared and spoken. On Lenin street the Horizont Russian bookshop had been broken into, and all its books brought out and burnt on the pavement. At *Szabad Nép*, where Mrs Gara had gone, the Hungarian tri-colour hung from the front of the building, the imitation Soviet coat of arms cut from the middle. No-one knew where Stephen was but he had been there a couple of hours before, the other printers assured her. Making her way home, Mrs Gara had seen armed men in lorries tearing around the streets. The insurrection had begun.

The next morning Stephen came home. In his pocket he carried a pistol. The bullets he had wrapped in a dirty piece of rag.

*   *   *

The next day was Wednesday. Stephen told Teresa not to go to school. He walked with her to buy bread. In the streets they passed two burning cars. Everywhere there were crowds of people standing around, looking and waiting.

A lorry passed filled with young men. They carried rifles, and wore bandoleers filled with bullets. The people on the pavement cheered.

From a piece of scaffolding a shop's dummy hung by the neck like a corpse on the gallows. On the placard nearby was written simply ERNO, the Christian name of the current Party Secretary. Portraits of Rákosi and Stalin smouldered on a fire in the middle of the intersection where the tram stop was. Everywhere there were flags: black flags and the Hungarian tri-colour, all with a porthole in the middle from where the imitation Soviet coat of arms had been cut.

On the other side of the courtyard, an AVO man lived with his mother. He did not wear a uniform; he operated in plain clothes. In the evening Stephen went over with three other men, taking the gun.

Teresa later learnt they found the man packing his suitcase. There was a scuffle. He escaped. The stairs were blocked by curious neighbours who had come to see what was happening. The AVO man ran up on to the roof, which unusually was flat, and Stephen and the men chased after him.

From the window of their room, Teresa and her mother could just see the outlines of scrambling figures on the other side. They lifted the window in order to see better.

Stephen and his friends caught the AVO man. They took him behind a chimney stack where they were hidden from sight. In the absolute silence, the AVO man could be heard crying and begging for his life. It was then Teresa noticed there was a huge crowd in the courtyard looking up and waiting, some sitting even on the wooden frame used for beating carpets, and almost every window on her side was open and with someone hanging out of it.

There was a dull bang as the gun went off. Stephen and the other men appeared, pulling the corpse over the flat roof. They heaved it over the edge and it fell into the courtyard.

The next morning Teresa passed the AVO man lying on his back. Someone had put a portrait of Stalin on the ground beside him and it looked as if the two were in conversation. Someone else had been through the dead man's pockets, found one of his wage slips and pinned it to the lapel of his tunic. Teresa didn't look at this small piece of paper but from the mutterings of those standing round and looking, she gathered the AVO man had earned many thousands of *forints* a month. Her father didn't even earn a thousand.

The dead man's eyes were open but the pupils had rolled back so only the whites showed. The night before, the event on the roof had seemed unreal but now there was no doubt – someone was dead. Teresa was glad she didn't know who'd pulled the trigger behind the chimney stack. She hurried on.

Two weeks later, exactly, there was a Soviet tank at the end of their street, just where the tram stop was. Stephen, who had been printing underground tracts and broadsheets for the resistance, was now out of action. Jumping down from a lorry, he had wrenched his ankle, tearing the cartilage. He wrapped his pistol in scraps of old blanket and a sheet of rubber he had found somewhere, and hobbled down the stairs in the middle of the night and hid it in the building's cellar.

The same night Mrs Gara packed a small suitcase. The original intention had been that they would all leave together, but now that Stephen could no longer walk properly – and they knew there would be long distances to cover on foot when they reached the Austrian border – there had been a change of plan. Teresa was to leave with Sándor immediately; Stephen and Mária would follow. Somehow, they would get across the border at a later date.

Into the suitcase Mrs Gara put Teresa's two dresses and her two pairs of stockings. Teresa put on what she wore to school and, underneath the skirt, a pair of trousers for extra warmth. A neighbour provided a pair of felt-lined boots and, wearing three pairs of thick socks, Teresa could just fill them out.

At midnight, Sándor slipped into the room. Teresa was sitting between her mother and father on their bed, holding each one by the hand. She had her coat on and the suitcase was on the chair.

She embraced her mother and father and saw Sándor was already standing in the doorway holding her suitcase. It had arrived: the moment to say goodbye. She felt a pain in the back of her throat but when she opened her mouth to speak, it was a trembling croak which came out and not a word.

She felt Sándor taking her by the arm and pulling her. In a moment she was outside at the top of the dark stairs, and all the tears which she felt she had been filling up with suddenly started to flow, and she could feel salty streaks running down her cheek.

She turned and saw her mother and father standing in the doorway of their room. They were side by side, not touching. The light was behind them and she could not see their faces. She ran her tongue under her nose. It was wet and it tasted of salt.

Sándor tugged again. She followed after him and a moment later she was in darkness with a great pain in the middle of her chest and tears streaming from her eyes. She could not see where she was going and she let Sándor guide her.

There was an ambulance outside, filled with children and young people. The road west was choked with refugees and it took two days to reach the vicinity of the border. A guide led the party overland for the last ten miles, through fields filled with snow and across freezing rivers.

Teresa and the party she was with reached a reception camp on the Austrian side in the early hours of the morning. It was filled with thousands of other Hungarian refugees.

She had nothing – she had lost her suitcase in the countryside – except for the little gourd pipe her father had brought home from the war. It was in the pocket of her coat. Waiting to be processed, she fingered it continuously. Later she slept with it under her pillow. It was all that remained of home.

Back in Budapest, Kadar's new regime was installed. The ankle took weeks to heal properly, and by that time the border was closed. Stephen lost his job. He was put to sweeping the streets. After nine months he was allowed to return to his original trade, only now he was no longer at *Szabad Nép*; instead he was placed in a less prestigious concern, which printed local party material and provincial newspapers. The message of his reinstatement was unambiguous; Stephen knew that from then on his status was never going to improve, and the possibility of his ever being granted a passport was now out of the question. In the years which followed, he became morose and unhappy; a man who just survived, living his life out day by day, without hope. No-one was really surprised when, a fortnight after the Soviet invasion of Czechoslovakia, he threw himself under a tram and was decapitated.

Diary, Hampton Wick

The whole family gathered in the kitchen. There was champagne which fizzled in the mouth and we ate scrambled eggs with strips of crispy bacon. It was Eva's favourite breakfast but she hardly touched her plate. Nor did she say much except "please" and "thank you".

The effect of the drink was to make us all louder and certainly more cheerful than usual. This did not seem to please Eva. Sometimes, out of the corner of my eye, I thought I caught an expression of disgust on her face, to remind me that she was loathing our high spirits.

When we had finished, Teresa cleared away the plates and slipped outside with that peculiar look of self-effacement which I have seen at a hundred birthday parties before what came next. True enough, two or three minutes later, the door leading from the hall opened and there she stood. She was holding a cake with twenty-one candles burning on top of it. The flames looked pale in the daylight.

Everyone said, "Whey", although I noticed Eva was scowling.

The confectioner's silver tray and the cake on top went down on the table. It was a chocolate cake with white piping. There were twenty-one candles on it and written on it in red icing was "Eva-Happiest-21st".

Eva filled her lungs with air. Teresa stood ready with her Instamatic camera. Everyone waited. Eva expelled the air from her lungs with a loud puff. Teresa clicked. Every candle went out. We cheered. After a moment, little silver sparks shot from the candle ends and suddenly little buds of flame sprung up around the wicks.

"Oh no, not the magic candles," said Eva morosely.

Everyone laughed.

"Go on," urged Malachy, "see if you can get them out."

"I'm not going to play this game."

She pulled at the candle nearest her, and when it came away, a large skein of icing on which the letter "E" of "Eva" was resting came away with it. She dropped the lot into her champagne glass. What looked like fragments of burnt paper floated down from the wick through her champagne.

"Twenty, I can do twenty," shouted her brother, ignoring the damage, and he gave a huge puff.

The candles died and then a moment later they sparked and re-lit.

"Come on," he called to me and together we blew.

"Yes," said Teresa cheerfully, "it looks like you've done it." She added, "Here Eva darling." She had fetched a clean glass and filled it with champagne which she now passed to her daughter.

The candle wicks sparked and caught fire again.

"This is ridiculous," moaned Eva. She blew a short, savage burst of air at the cake and stood up holding her glass.

"OK," said Malachy with a shrug, "Eva doesn't like them, so the candles must go."

He started to pluck them one by one and threw them on to a plate.

"Sit down," said Eva's father in his most coaxing tone of voice. It was the first time he'd spoken at that breakfast. He tugged gently on her wrist and with a shrug she let herself drop back to her seat.

"Very nice champagne," he said. He toasted Eva silently. She didn't respond but stared intently and sullenly at the table top.

"I like the old bubbly," John continued with a smile, which I took to be his reaction to his daughter's petulance. "How's the bottle?" He tilted back his chair and took it out of the sink where it had been standing in cold water. He lifted it across – great drops splattering from it on to the table top like rain – and poured the remainder into his daughter's glass.

"I think we'll have another," he said and winked at me because I was the one closest to the refrigerator.

I got out the bottle and started to peel off the silver foil. On top of the cake there were twenty neat rounds like bird marks in the snow and a gash where the icing had been pulled away.

"You've got to hold the knife upside-down and make a wish," I head Malachy saying. I took off the wire which held the cork fast.

"Do I have to?" asked Eva, her arms hanging down by the side of her black dress, the knife held limply in her left hand. Behind her hair, the earrings which Malachy had given her gleamed faintly.

"Yes, enter into the spirit, you know – contribute," Teresa said, speaking brightly to take the sting out of the last word. "How often are you twenty-one?"

Eva sighed and said tartly, "Once."

"Once, that's right," Malachy added cheerfully. "Hold the knife upside-down, make the cut, make your wish."

John turned the knife round in his daughter's hand. Malachy covered Eva's eyes with the palm of his hand. John guided Eva's hand holding the knife to the cake.

"Don't tell us your wish," Teresa said.

"I know, Mother, don't tell me, I know. For God's sake, how old do you think I am?"

I twisted the cork in the mouth of the bottle.

John said, "One, two, three . . ."

Eva limply pushed the knife down.

The cork came out but instead of a pop there was only a slow hiss. The others cheered. Teresa took the knife from her daughter.

"All right," she said, "everyone wants a slice, a big slice. Today, to hell with cholesterol and calories."

She cut a large wedge and lifted it on to a plate.

I went out to the hall and fetched the present which I had for Eva but which I hadn't yet given to her. It was what she had asked for. I returned and she tore off the paper listlessly and took out the pair of black leather gloves inside.

"Thank you," she said but she didn't stand. She waited with her head tilted sideways for me to kiss her cheek. I bent forward and for a second, before my lips brushed her skin, I caught her glance. She looked to me as if she were completely mad. I kissed her quickly and stood up.

The neighbours from next door, Henry and Paul, appeared,

with a bunch of red and blue roses from their garden. As we hadn't any more chairs, they sat on the draining board on either side of the sink, drinking champagne, their hairy legs hanging down from their shorts.

Peake came soon after and brought a gingham dress for Eva and a fifties' picnic set with blue bakelite plates and stainless steel cutlery. It came packed in a heavy green box the size of an old portable gramophone.

At ten o'clock, John fetched the car out of the garage. The tank was almost empty and he went off to get petrol.

Waiting, I found myself in the hall with Eva. She was standing in front of the mirror staring at herself. I sat on the bottom step of the stairs, relacing a shoe. Every now and again I glanced at her reflection, and tried to see if the terrible expression which had been there at breakfast was still showing. I couldn't see it.

"What did you wish?" It was an idle question, asked because there was time to kill and I couldn't think of anything else to talk about.

"To be in cold storage."

"What?"

"To be in one of those huge refrigerators for a few months and to be just completely out of it."

A few minutes later we all crammed into the car. I was in the back. Teresa was in the front by her husband with the *A–Z* open on her lap.

"OK, off we go," he said.

"Did we lock the kitchen window?" Teresa asked.

"Yes Mum, I did, no-one's going to get in," said Malachy from the back.

We started the journey. We all talked except for Eva who stared out of the window. We speculated as to whether the pilot would take us on a series of heart-stopping loop-the-loops or perhaps under Tower bridge.

"Hasn't that gone?" asked Eva abruptly.

"No, no, you're getting mixed up with London bridge," her brother said.

Our progress out of town was slow because of the traffic.

Later, when we got out into the approximation of countryside which surrounds the city, there was less of it and we speeded up. The steady hum of the engine had a mesmerising effect and we all stopped talking.

Our silence continued, until we reached the gates of the commercial aerodrome from which we were going to make our flight. We turned through and were directed by a commissionaire to the car park.

When I got out I saw a cream-coloured building, which looked as if it had been built in the thirties. There was a control tower sitting on top of it. Inside this were a couple of air traffic controllers. The runway beyond was a sort of yellow colour and along the margins stood three huge corrugated sheds from which aeroplanes with propellers stuck out.

We filed into the cream-coloured building, and went to the Club room. It smelt of stale beer and cigarettes. There was a bar decorated with plastic warplanes which hung from pieces of thread, behind which a middle-aged man with a handlebar moutstache was stacking bottles. He told John the bar was shut and pointed to the vending machine.

We sat at the table by the long window which overlooked the runway, with tepid cups of tea and coffee which we had got from the machine. Teresa had a packet of Kwells – "Guaranteed to eliminate nausea at sea and in the air" – which she offered around. Everyone declined except, strangely, Eva. John fumed at not being able to get an alcoholic drink and ended by saying, "The English, they're such bloody killjoys." Peake went off to see what was happening and came back with the news that our plane was being refuelled.

Fifteen minutes later the pilot appeared. He was a small, dapper man with a beard, carrying a clipboard. His blue trousers, blue shirt, blue jersey – and to complete the effect, blue peaked hat – together gave a military impression.

He unfolded an enormous map and laid it on the table. It was London, the Thames coloured blue, wriggling through the middle, and the main roads, coloured orange, dividing the city into sections.

The pilot said, "By the way, my name's Fred," and clicked his pen several times as if to get our attention.

We all bent forward.

"This is the route we shall be following," and with the end of his pen he described our flight path.

Eva followed his description, which was lengthy and complicated but when he'd finished said, "Where did you say we're going?" as if she hadn't been able to absorb a word he'd said.

After he'd been through it again, we followed him outside. There was a wind blowing and a strong smell of fuel. Lengths of metal hawser coiled like serpents lay on the grass at the side.

Fred pointed with his clipboard at a hangar and purposefully started heading towards it. A turbo-prop aeroplane accelerated down the runway and we stopped to watch it taking off and then stayed watching it as it circled overhead.

"Come on," Fred said when it disappeared into the cloud and we walked on.

A second turbo-prop appeared and taxied down the runway towards us. Raised high on its front wheels and falling back to the ground at an extraordinary angle, the propellers in the middle of each wing slowly turning, it made me think of pterodactyls and dinosaurs and all the other reptiles which had died out in prehistoric times. In the cockpit I noticed a figure was sitting.

We went on. The aeroplane came to a halt. When it was not far away, say the distance from one side of the street in Hampton Wick to the other, Eva ran ahead of us and started turning, holding her arms out. Her hair rose as she spun.

"This feels so good," she shouted.

Fred looked at her as he passed but he didn't stop. "I'm very glad to hear that," he called back to her. He sounded embarrassed.

Eva spun again and again, moving away from our path and out on to the runway. The pilot in the cockpit of the aeroplane had put on dark glasses and was reading something.

"Hey, not that way," Fred called after Eva. She adjusted her course, whirled back towards us, and then suddenly looped away again towards the aeroplane.

"Eva," Teresa called, with just the faintest edge of anxiety in her voice, "you heard the man. Come back."

Eva, deaf to her mother's calls, went on spinning. I could just hear her high-pitched thin cries over the roar of the engines.

She was a dozen feet from the wing tip. My arm stretched in front of me, as if I were about to offer a dance. Eva lifted her dress and darted forward on her brown, bandy legs at an extraordinary speed.

"Eva," the others called. The pilot could not hear them over the roar of the engines.

We stood still, transfixed.

She was someone about to step through a curtain and on to a stage.

If only she would turn round and see their faces, I thought, her mother's and father's and her brother's and Peake's; that would dissuade her. I wanted to call out, "I love you", but when I opened my mouth nothing came out.

The pilot began to turn his head.

Eva must have seen him for, an instant later, she bent forward, like someone about to go through a low door, and stepped into the propeller.

Her body and the blades merged and seemed to stand still and then a small drop of metallic-tasting blood landed on my lip.

London. I was driving John's Sierra. From Paddington I turned on to the part of the Harrow road running underneath the Westway, a small section of urban motorway where there are only cars and never pedestrians. Suddenly I saw Eva standing by the side of the road. She was wearing the kaftan which she had come home with, on the morning I had tried to leave the house, and her expression, from what I could see, was untroubled. What's she doing there? I wondered. There was a car stopped not far from her and there was a man with it. I didn't entirely like the look of him. Do I stop? I wondered and then I thought, She wouldn't be there unless she meant to be there. I went on and disappeared down into the tunnel.

Later, when I got back to the house in Hampton Wick, I found Teresa distraught. She told me her daughter had been murdered by the man who'd been fiddling with the car at the very place where I had passed her . . .

I woke from this nightmare but kept my eyes closed. There was a moment of stillness when I knew there was something I had forgotten which was wanting to be remembered. I knew at the same time I must not remember. The longer I could procrastinate, the better.

My heart started to beat faster as I felt more and more fearful about what was pressing to be recalled. Let it come out and let's get this over with, came a renegade thought. My concentration wavered and what had been deferred pushed forward. This was the day we were going to bury Eva.

Straight away, the feelings which I had been free from during the night and during those first few seconds returned. The back of my throat felt sore, just the way it used to when I cried as a child, although now the feeling came even though I didn't or couldn't cry. I felt a sharp, eerie pain in the place in the middle of the body where feelings gather. I felt a terrible lassitude, as if I could sleep for ever, yet I knew that if I had been in a position just to lie in my bed all day, sleep would never have come.

I opened my eyes and made myself listen. The only way to manage in this situation was involvement with the world. Rain was falling outside. Droplets knocked against the glass but where it fell on the leaves of the trees and the bushes, it produced a whispering "ssss" sound.

I lifted back the covers and went to look out the window. Below me stretched the garden. The earth of the flowerbeds was dark, almost black, and the lawn, no longer green, was a depressing dun colour.

The weather, to which normally I would not really have paid much attention, increased my feeling of despondency, and then I noticed the badminton net sagging with the weight of absorbed wet. I had forgotten to bring it in, I realised, which I had promised Teresa I would do, and my omission struck me as a calamitous oversight. I thought of Avril. I had to get round to her.

I got dressed and went downstairs intending to get my coat in the hall.

"You're up very early."

Teresa was in the living room and the door was open. She was in her dressing gown and her legs were crossed. One or two blue twists of vein showed on her shins.

"I forgot to bring in the net last night," I said, remembering it again.

"I couldn't sleep."

Teresa had haunted the house every early morning since Eva's death.

I asked, "Do you want anything?"

She shook her head.

I skirted the ping-pong table and went through the sliding door into the garden. It was cold and blustery and the wind was sighing in the boughs of the apple trees. I felt the rain on my cheeks.

The knots holding up the badminton net were wet and tight. I had to unpick them with a nail. I rolled it up and brought it in and left it in the laundry room, a sodden, oozing heap smelling faintly of string.

Back in the hall I found Teresa was where I had left her. She was in the big square front living room in the armchair in front of the door.

"I'm going out now. For a walk," I said, dread stirring faintly that she might ask me to stay and talk. We had done so much lately I doubted I could find anything more in myself to say. I shouldn't have worried because all she came back with in reply was a very faraway sounding, "Oh."

She tipped a length of ash from the cigarette she was smoking on to the ashtray on her lap. She had started again at the aerodrome after ten years without.

She glanced at the window and said, "It's raining still."

"I'll be back soon," I said and kissed the side of her head.

I took my coat off the hook and slipped outside. There had been a storm in the night. Bits of debris from the monkey-puzzle tree all over the garden, and on the corner of Dyson avenue, the plum tree which overhung the pavement had shed most of its fruit. They lay around everywhere, and many of those in the road had already been splattered by passing cars, to form little blots on the tarmac.

I went on, moving fast but automatically through the empty,

wet streets. Every gutter seemed to be filled with swollen leaves and every drain to be choked with them.

I came at last to the red pillar box which marked the turning into Avril's street. I had spent many hours since the death in her house. We had sat mostly in the small front room. I had listened mostly and she had talked and sniffled and endlessly wiped her nose until it was red. I had rushed over impelled by the dream of us two throwing ourselves together but now I was only a few steps away, I saw this was a terrible mistake. I associated Avril so closely with Eva, she could only have worsened the ache and could not possibly have lessened it.

I turned round and started running. I ran and ran until I felt a stabbing sensation between my lungs. I stopped. I was in a street of large brick buildings. I recognised one of them as Copperfield house from the time I'd returned the bag to Cindy.

A minute or so later and I was at her front door. I pressed the bell and waited. Nothing happened. I pressed the bell again. Footsteps slapped along the floor on the other side of the wood and a voice called out, "Hang on."

The door opened and there she stood. She was wearing the same nylon housecoat she'd been wearing before. Her peroxide hair was tangled and wisps stuck out in all directions.

She screwed up her eyes and she looked at my face. I was just about to remind her that we'd once met, when her expression changed and she said, "Oh yeah." She'd remembered.

I went in and she closed the door.

I didn't feel I was present but was watching someone just like myself.

She went down the dark corridor and opened a door.

"Are you all right Daniel?" she asked.

I took two steps forward and over her shoulder just caught a glimpse of the corner of a cot and a teddy bear on the floor.

A child said, "Yes."

"I'll make your breakfast in a minute. Now you be a good boy and play quietly."

She closed the door and then surreptitiously turned the key in the lock so the child inside wouldn't hear.

"In there," she said to me and pointed towards another door.

I went through. There was a bed with a buttoned burgundy-coloured velvet headboard and net curtains over the windows. A glass mobile tinkled somewhere. On the dressing table there was a large framed photograph of Daniel.

I got a twenty-pound note out in readiness and buttoned up the wallet in the back pocket of my trousers. The only thing which I can remember about that moment is the vague anxiety which I had that I might be robbed.

A lavatory flushed. The door opened and she came in, her housecoat trailing after her. I handed over the money. She said nothing. There's no turning back now, I thought.

She opened a drawer in her dressing table. Inside was a cigar box into which she put the money. She shut the drawer again and came over to me.

"Half and half."

It could have been a question or a statement. I had no idea what she meant but I said, "Yes."

She took off her clothes. She was wearing a pair of stockings which supported themselves of their own accord. She was very white and plump, especially at the tops of her thighs and around her bottom. She sat down on the bed. Between her legs her pubic hair was black.

"Come here," she said.

Her body was a series of curves which merged one into the other. I took off my coat and stepped over to her. She undid the buckle of my belt and pulled down my trousers and my boxer shorts as far as my knees. She took my penis and put it straight into her mouth.

When it was erect but keeping it in her mouth, she pulled open the drawer of her bedside bureau and took out a small silver package. She tore it open and the unmistakable rubber smell of the prophylactic inside drifted up.

She moved her head back and slipped the sheath over the tip.

"You don't mind do you?" she asked.

I didn't say a thing.

She lay back on the bed. I got on top of her and between her legs.

She reached down and a moment later I felt the warmth and

knew she had pulled me into her. She got her hands under my shirt and began to run her fingernails up and down my spine.

I could feel her stocking tops chafing my thighs. I buried my face into her neck, her hair and the bedclothes. My hips went backwards and forwards. I heard her saying, "Ohh", and "Ahh", and wondered in a vague way if they were for real or fake. Vague images of the female body, and of Eva, floated into my mind. Later it was just Eva. I came and surprised myself by letting out a small quiet cry.

"Better now?" she asked.

I don't remember what I said but I know I withdrew and stood up. By the time I had buckled my belt, she was back in her night clothes.

She followed me out into the hall. While I waited by the front door near the poster I had noticed on my first visit, of the three cats playing with the ball of wool, she stopped in front of her child's door and silently unlocked it.

"Have my number," she said.

Before I could answer, she had taken a card out of her pocket which she gave to me. It read *Simply Cindy* and gave a telephone number below.

She opened the front door and I slipped out.

"Goodbye," she called. "Take care. See you soon. Look after yourself," and the door shut.

I threw the card down a drain and went home. I found Teresa sitting where I had left her. She was smoking another cigarette.

"I'm back. Hello."

She smiled and said, "There's some coffee in the kitchen."

That was the moment when I remembered I hadn't taken off the contraceptive but before I could rush off, Teresa lifted her cup and saucer towards me and wanly said, "Can you bring me some more?"

I walked across the room transfixed by the idea it was going to tumble out the bottom of a trouser leg.

It didn't and when I got to the kitchen I wrapped it in tissue paper ready to be flushed away.

I returned with Teresa's coffee and one for myself. We drank without speaking. The ache, the trickle of pain, the feeling of lassitude; everything I had woken with, it was all unchanged, as if nothing had happened, as if there'd been no Cindy, nothing . . .

After the service in the church, the undertakers carried the coffin out to the car. We drove in procession through the country lanes of Sussex to a large cemetery. The O'Neills had no connection with this part of the country. We were here simply because it was the first place they could get a plot.

We parked the cars and the undertakers carried the coffin to the hole which had been dug. We stood and listened as the priest read from the Bible. It was overcast but it was not raining any longer. The earth which had been taken out to make the hole was black and wet and had adhered into lumps.

It was an enormous place with hundreds of graves stretching in all directions, and black and white cows in a field beyond a distant wall. We were the only people there. Then I noticed an oldish woman had come in and made her way to the grave two or three plots to the side of us. She had come with a watering can and slopped water out on to the pathway where she put it down, and she had a bunch of flowers to replace the dead withered stalks in the urn in front of the headstone. She got down on to her knees, grumbling and sighing loudly to herself, and magically produced a trowel out of her pocket. With this she started to hack and scrape along the border of the grave, where a few small weeds had managed to spring up. Something made her angry because she started scouring with the trowel fiercely, making a loud noise. I wondered if anyone in our party had heard or been disturbed by her and turned back to see but no-one appeared to have noticed her. Now I looked at them all closely, as they stood there in their black clothes, John, Teresa, Peake, Malachy, Avril and Mrs Gara and I noticed, which I hadn't seen before, that they were all looking intently at the same spot – the hole.

The priest stopped and the undertakers lowered the coffin on ropes. As it swung down it banged against the sides of the grave. It didn't look to me as though they were having to lower something terribly heavy and it crossed my mind that it might be nearly empty. But I knew that couldn't be true. I had heard John on the telephone giving instructions to the undertakers concerning the remains.

The priest nodded. Malachy went round to the foot of the grave, picked up a handful of earth and tossed it down. When it landed on the coffin lid it made a noise like stones rolling across a slate roof.

Malachy filed away and John led his wife over by the arm. He dropped down at the knees, and picked up a handful of earth. He let it trickle down out of his fingers and the noise like stones on a roof again rose from below.

Teresa, keeping one hand on his arm, started bending down in the same way that her husband had towards the ground. Half-way there she stopped and let out a short sob and it was clear she wasn't going to be able to manage fetching her own handful of earth.

John lifted her up and stood her on her feet. He carefully removed her hand from his arm. He squatted down and scooped a big handful of earth with both palms, then stood up again and offered the earth which he had to Teresa. She looked at him and he nodded at her several times to encourage her to reach out and take some. I don't know how long this went on for. It seemed like minutes but it was probably only seconds.

Teresa reached forward finally, and took a handful in each fist. Her lip began to quiver. There was another pause. Suddenly, she raised both her arms over her head and then dashed them down with a terrible shriek, at the same time letting go of the earth she had. It scattered everywhere: downwards; sideways over all of us; forwards; even upwards. Two graves away, the woman with the trowel looked round and stared open-mouthed.

Teresa dropped on to her knees. No one moved. The whole morning which had glided by like something in a dream suddenly became real at that moment. I knew that now I was going to feel worse, which was almost unimaginable, but that that was also for the better. Those feelings which the event would trigger I was going to feel now; not a day, a month or a year hence.

Through the tears in my eyes I saw Teresa crawling forward. When she got to the edge of the hole, she peered down as if she were curious. She let out a terrible cry of anguish and started to slump forward, making as if to slither down on to the wood below. John jumped forward and took her by the shoulders. She tried to shrug his hands away. He must have tightened his grip because he wouldn't be shaken off. He started to pull her back and up on to her knees. She flailed with her arms and waved her head violently from side to side. He got his arms under her armpits and started pulling. Teresa scrambled madly with her feet. Earth scattered everywhere. One of her black court shoes came off, flew over the edge and landed on the coffin with a hollow thud. I felt the first tear roll down my cheek and settle on my lip. I wiped it away with the back of my hand. I had a sudden perception then which I'd never had before. What made a funeral terrible was not the dead, or the death alone; it was the conjunction of the living and the dead and the fact that after it was over, the living would have to go on existing with their loss for the rest of their lives. Death didn't bother the dead. We, the living, were its victims.

John had managed to get Teresa on to her feet. Leaning heavily on his arms and sobbing, she hopped with him on the foot which still had a shoe, across the grass and down the path.

Malachy lay down on the ground and reached forward. He got her shoe off the coffin and went after his parents with it. He put the shoe down on the concrete and turned round and came back to the grave.

Teresa lifted her leg and started trying to brush off the earth and the bits of grass which had stuck to the bottom of her black-stockinged foot.

She didn't seem to be able to shift much. She stopped, dropped her leg and went to find her shoe with her foot. "Lean here. I'll do it," said John. Holding on to his shoulder, she lifted her leg again, and he began to brush away the bits of earth and debris stuck there.

Epilogue

That's right. You've guessed. This is not Malachy from America speaking. This is Malachy from London speaking – or should I say writing?

Last term we were given a project – Home. There were no other choices; that was it. "Explore the concept," the tutor said to all of us, "in whatever way you wish. I'm sure with diligence every one of you will be able to create a little niche for yourselves."

I had an inspiration. Malachy had kept a diary. If I could get it, I could use it as a basis. I rang him up. He agreed. I suppose he's the sort of person who's got to tell the truth. It arrived. I read it. I must say, he hadn't pulled his punches.

I decided to use his stuff as my raw material. I edited, rearranged, revised. I put in stories about my ancestors which he wasn't in a position to know about. I spent the whole of Christmas typing it up (and it was just as well I had something to do because this was our first without Eva and it was awful. Just myself, the parents and Grandma Gara, oh God). When I took the typescript in at the start of the next term, my tutor and the college weren't entirely delighted that my submission was just a written text. But after they'd read some, they changed their minds. I hope to do well from it but I'm going to have to add some visual material to support it.

Malachy, the name, came from my father's maternal grandfather, James Malachy Garrett, the one who fled from Kildare to Donegal with his family after being evicted. Father's first (Ameri-

can) wife Amy and he had always agreed, if they had a son, this
would be his name. When Malachy was born in America, Amy
decided to stick with this. It was pretty funny when you think
about it, because she was passing off the baby at the time as her
second husband's. Of course, the real father was John O'Neill.
She must have still felt attached. What I wonder is, did she tell her
new husband where the name came from? Or did she just say, "I
like it honey, it's weird but nice."

The one thing you can't say about Mum and Dad is that they
kept the skeleton of Malachy hidden from us. I can't remember
how or when I was told but I know I knew about my half-
brother from almost as far back as I can remember, and I knew
what he was called.

Sharing this odd name which no-one else had, I often used to
think about him when I was a child. I can clearly remember
sitting on the window ledge of my bedroom on summer's
evenings, looking down into the garden and trying to imagine his
life. I used to do a lot of day dreaming in this position. Just
looking at the lawn below and the shadows of the apple trees
spreading across it would still my mind so that the pictures could
start rising up.

I would see him with my inner eye, lying in his bed in the early
morning. I would see him opening his eyes and looking around
his room. I would see him seeing a poster on the wall of a suitable
American scene, like a man swinging a baseball bat, or of
Abraham Lincoln. I would see him climbing out of bed and
going to the window. I would see what he saw: a small garden
with washing hanging from a dryer like an inverted pyramid of
wire, and beyond a road of white suburban houses with big
American cars parked in the driveways.

Next I would see him going downstairs. He would sit at the
table in the kitchen. He would eat a bowl of cereal or an egg. He
would leave the house shouting "Goodbye". He would walk
along the street or get into the back of one of those big American
cars. Someone vague – I always had difficulty picturing anyone

but him — would drive him to school. He'd get out. There'd be children milling about, all saying, "Oh, yeah", and chewing gum. A bell would sound. Everyone would start to move towards the school steps . . .

At this point I would stop and return to the front of the story again. I could never get further than the school bell. To go further would have meant going inside, and that would have meant a teacher, other children, relationships. It was hard enough, because I had never been to America, picturing the physical world, but to picture a world of fully rounded people was beyond me. Then I got a brilliant inspiration.   Bizarro world — one of the more exotic inventions in *Superman* — is a copy of planet Earth in the fourth dimension, only the copy hasn't come off. The cars are not purring, gleaming pieces of advanced engineering, as in Metropolis, they are clapped-out rusting wrecks, held together with pieces of string and elastoplast, and instead of round wheels, they have square ones. The apartment blocks are not towering monuments to modern architecture, as in Metropolis; they are half-collapsed, semi-derelict buildings, with broken windows, doors which don't shut properly and dangerous fire escapes. One image which I never forgot from the comics was the picture of a Bizarro-world cafeteria with a neon sign outside which read *Don't Eat Here*. Bizarro world was like a third-world America with all the bits — the automobiles, the air-conditioning units, the Cadillacs — but gone decrepit, turned to junk, and back to front.

Inhabiting this world are Bizarro people. They are replicas of people from earth. Jimmy Olson, Lois Lane, even Superman — the whole gallery of characters from Metropolis are there. But like the environment, the replication has gone very wrong. The people look as though they've been made out of clay which has been left too long in the kiln and has cracked. Their talk is primitive: "Me Superman. Me heap hungry."

I appropriated the Bizarro world/Earth relationship, and added my brother. The way I conceived our balance was not literally but in such terms that if one of us was having good fortune, the other automatically would be having bad fortune. If my life was going well, his would necessarily be going badly. The next stage followed logically. I started to think that for me to do well, he would have to do badly, and vice versa. I was plunged into a world of acute ethical dilemma. Every wish and indeed every achievement was balanced on the other side of the globe by the other Malachy being thwarted or failing. Conversely, when I failed at something or something went wrong for me, he would be succeeding at what he wanted, or something would be going well for him.

One day I saw how ridiculous it was and I just stopped. From that day on, although I sometimes thought about this curious episode, I never told anyone about it. It stayed a secret until one day I told the doctor. She was fascinated. After I had finished, I could hear her scribbling furiously in her notebook.

"How do you view this childhood fantasy now?" she asked, and she returned to it time after time in our subsequent sessions. Now I think I know why. Clearly, I was not on one side of an invisible weighing scales as a child and he on the other. When I was at the dentist having a tooth drilled it was implausible that he was automatically eating candy-floss. In other words, when I had those fantasies I was sustaining a view of the world contradicted by all the evidence but which, none the less, was true for me. This must have been Eva's condition, which is what I think the psychiatrist wanted me to see. It has its origins in both her life and her past. There was bad blood on both sides of the family and it was her bad luck to get both strains together.

On the other hand, you can't know everything about a person. There was an "X" in her, like there is in all of us. If it could be taken out, put under a microscope and cut into slivers, we wouldn't be human.

I'll never understand her act, or anything, not fully, but I must never give up trying.

I talked to the psychiatrist about this once. "Yes," she said. "You're talking about the eternal paradox of man's condition. He seeks to know and knows he never will.

"Do you know about the medieval Christian concept of the maze?"

"No."

"You'll find many medieval churches have a maze drawn on

the ground in front of the altar. These are mazes of incredible complexity. To follow them through to the centre takes almost for ever. One aspect of private worship was to begin to follow the maze. To run one's eye along it. The end was never reached and the point for the supplicant was this lesson. It's the progression that matters, not reaching the goal. Am I making sense?"

Then she said. "Why don't you write it down. Write down what happened."

I'd already started. I was one step ahead of her there.

I left the manuscript on the kitchen table a fortnight ago. There was a note with it. 'Read this.' My father said nothing when he'd finished with it. My mother was red eyed afterwards.

I think of us as crabs, each in our own shell.

I'm going to America next summer. I've made the arrangements. I'm going to stay with my half-brother. I will be met at the airport in Newark, New Jersey. I may never come back. Malachy is going to marry Avril.

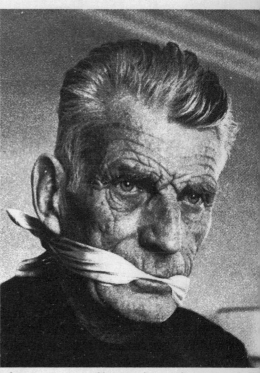